P.A. Ross

The Birth of Vengeance: Vampire Formula #1

P.A. Ross

SCARLETT-THORN
PUBLISHING

http://www.thornsneedles.com/

Copyright © 2012 By P.A. Ross

Scarlett-Thorn Publishing

11th Edition

This is a work of fiction. Names, characters, businesses, places, events, locales, and incidents are either the products of the author's imagination or used in a fictitious manner. Any resemblance to actual persons, living or dead, or actual events is purely coincidental

All rights reserved.
ISBN-13: 978-1479192526

TABLE OF CONTENTS

PROLOGUE 1
CHAPTER ONE 1
CHAPTER TWO 9
CHAPTER THREE 17
CHAPTER FOUR 22
CHAPTER FIVE 33
CHAPTER SIX 41
CHAPTER SEVEN 46
CHAPTER EIGHT 49
CHAPTER NINE 57
CHAPTER TEN 61
CHAPTER ELEVEN 65
CHAPTER TWELVE 73
CHAPTER THIRTEEN 84
CHAPTER FOURTEEN 92
CHAPTER FIFTEEN 98
CHAPTER SIXTEEN 106
CHAPTER SEVENTEEN 112
CHAPTER EIGHTEEN 121
CHAPTER NINETEEN 126
CHAPTER TWENTY 132
CHAPTER TWENTY-ONE 137
CHAPTER TWENTY-TWO 143

PROLOGUE

Jonathan Harper had to die for me to live.

CHAPTER ONE

I stared at the clock above the door while the seconds dragged on. The clock teased us with the slow progression of the minute hand, as Mr May droned on about revising over the half term. He rambled on, padding out the time with his briefcase packed and his brown blazer on, ready to leave. He glanced over to the clock before adjusting his glasses and sweeping back his thinning hair.

I sighed in painful boredom. No one ever listened to him. Instead, everyone would be mentally ticking off the time left, bit by painful bit, looking forward to the bell that would signal our freedom for one whole week.

I had arranged to meet Giles, my best friend, by the front gates at the end of the term. Giles and I had been friends since our first year at school, at five years old. This year would be our last year, as we approached our sixteenth birthdays.

We shared many of the same interests. We both loved sci-fi films and would watch entire trilogies in one sitting. Often we'd munch through bags of salt and vinegar crisps while checking out the movie trailers online for the forthcoming blockbusters.

During the dark evenings, we blasted each other through online games, not wanting to go out as the local area got rough. We lived near to a problem estate in Leeds, England, and often trouble would overflow into our neighbourhood.

That day, I had gained permission to go straight to Giles' house after school to play computer games, and my Dad would pick me up on his way home from work about midnight. Dad worked for the government in research, and his experiments meant he needed to work in the evenings. I never saw him that much, but it came in handy at times.

The hands on the clock ticked onwards, and I checked for the two computer games wedged at the bottom of my school bag. Yes, I felt their rectangle shapes jutting out.

The bell rang. I shoved my books into the bag, jumped up, grabbed my coat, put it on, and zipped it up tight. I swung my rucksack on and rushed to the door, pushing to get out as soon as possible. The classes across the school emptied into the corridors like cockroaches escaping the light, including the teachers who fought past the students to freedom. The air buzzed with laughter and chatter, as the excitement of the half term infected everyone's mood.

As I shuffled forward in the heaving crowd, I glimpsed pictures of school projects on the walls. The year's maths project on the uses of trigonometry in building houses and biology projects on the reproduction cycle of frogs. In the heaving crowd, the tatty "Code of Honour" poster got pulled down. It had been there for years, and I couldn't remember anyone reading it. The poster laid out rules on respecting each other and showing consideration, but I doubted if the teachers had even read it.

A young boy slipped up on the poster and fell to the floor. The crowd surged around him, stopping him from getting up. I stepped in behind and grabbed under both his arms and hauled him up. The boy dusted himself off and turned around. He smiled and then frowned as he caught sight of me. "Oh. Thanks, mate."

His friends had stopped and waited for him as he caught up. "Better hope no one saw you helped up by the soft kid," his friend said, and they rejoined the crowd trying to escape the school.

As we moved onwards, I imagined Giles waiting for me at the front gates, and I wished the crowd would get a move on. I flooded out with the mass of other students through the two large glass doors and into the small courtyard at the front of the school.

Behind me, the grey concrete monstrosity of school loomed and cast its shadow across the courtyard. I breathed in the cold winter's air and blew out a sigh of relief from escaping the dull, depressing atmosphere that it created. School is supposed to be a place of learning and enlightenment; my school was a study in survival.

The snows of the last week remained as determined lumps at the sides of the road and shadowy corners of the courtyard. Students quickly met with waiting friends and made final adjustments, pulling up their coats and wrapping up in gloves, hats, and scarves.

To the side of the courtyard, a road snaked from the rear car park and bike racks to the school front gates. Some students ran across the snaking road to a grassy bank and towards the lumps of snow created by the caretaker.

Soon, snowballs flew, and students ran through the open gates as their opponents chased them with icy ammunition, pelting them on the back as they ran. Some misfired into parked cars and others hit people who yelled.

The grey metal gates had been opened inwards, and I saw the name of the school, "St Teresa's," attached in red metal letters with names and faces scratched into the paintwork.

The O'Keefe gang stood outside the front gates, jostling some unfortunate victim. I looked elsewhere, knowing better than to get involved and so did everyone else, including Mr May in his silver Volvo Estate. He had driven along the snaking road, nudging through groups crossing the road and pushing cyclists along. He drove through the gates and pulled away onto the main road. As he left, he ignored the O'Keefe gang and their victim. He must have looked straight through them to check for a gap in the traffic but never hesitated before accelerating away.

Parent's cars lined the road outside, students clambered inside, and then drove off home. Again, the other students and parents ignored the gang as if the hooded tops had made them invisible.

I walked about halfway through the courtyard and stood to the side as other cars and bikes came from around the back of the building. Streaming around me, other students wrapped up and walked on in groups of friends. I scanned about for Giles, as I wanted to warm up, get to his house, and start on the gaming session, but I couldn't see him anywhere.

I looked back across the courtyard to the front doors. Still no sign of him. I spun around again to look at the front gates. I had avoided looking at the gang, but as I glanced around, I recognised the victim's green rucksack. Giles had a similar green backpack. I looked closer, hoping to see someone else, but my head dropped at the sight of Giles getting pushed from side-to-side between laughing gang members.

Patrick O'Keefe, from our school year, took centre stage orchestrating the bullying, showing off to his brothers and the other gang members. Patrick had short black gelled hair and a freckled face. His eyes were sunken and skin greasy through a diet of chips. The rest of the gang consisted of his older brothers, Liam and Kieran, and several other notorious kids from outside school.

Kieran and Liam were identical twins and looked similar to Patrick, but since leaving school last year, tattoos had covered their forearms, and their hair was a greasy chaotic mess. The gang were clothed in streetwear of hooded tops, dirty ripped jeans or tracksuit bottoms, and trainers. Patrick and his friend Dave wore the school uniform of black trousers, blazer, white shirt, and blue/gold striped tie. The tie had been put into a big fat knot, and they wore grubby white trainers instead of shoes.

I remembered this morning's registration when Giles and I continued to plot our gaming session. Patrick had overheard us from the desk behind and asked us what games we owned. We remained silent as he tried to harass us for information, not wanting to give anything away for fear of Patrick and his gang stealing my games. We had waited it out 'til the first bell, and then dashed out before he could get hold of us. It had annoyed him, or our silence signalled something worth stealing.

At the front gates, Patrick pushed Giles into other gang members who shoved him back into the circle. Giles spun around. His face pale and brown eyes stretched wide. His head darted about as he looked at the gang and to the outside of the circle for salvation. Kieran swiped Giles' hat off his head and stuck it in his own pocket. Liam then grabbed Giles in a headlock and messed up his light brown hair.

I scanned the courtyard, hoping someone else would come to his rescue. I wouldn't stand a chance against even one of the gang members. I still couldn't see any teachers or anybody else who wanted to get involved. Giles' eyes flicked to outside the gang for help, but he searched in vain until he spotted me. His eyes relaxed in relief as a look of recognition crossed his face.

I reluctantly walked over with heavy muscles and stomach burning in fear. I guessed I would receive a beating and would lose my computer games. The gang noticed the sudden change in Giles' emotions and scanned for its source. Liam spotted me, peeled off the side of the circle, and his dirty hands grasped the top of my shoulders.

"Look away," Liam said and shoved me backward.

I staggered back into other students who scurried away from the action. Giles stared at me. I took a big breath and walked forward again. "Leave him alone," I said.

Liam stepped in, swinging a punch to my stomach. My breath exploded out of my lungs, and I scrunched up in pain.

Liam leant over me and grunted into my ear. "I said, look away, Harper. Now get up and go home. I don't want to see your pathetic face again."

I stood up and looked around for help, hoping someone may have noticed, but the hooded tops remained invisible to everyone. Students, teachers, and parents all looked anywhere but at me.

A girl from my year placed her hand under my arm and pulled me up. "You best get some help, Jon. You can't win."

I turned to head back into school for help, but Liam blocked my path and pointed towards the main road. I dropped my eyes to the floor and scurried away. I accepted the command in the knowledge I had little choice, but I felt guilty having not tried harder, and even guiltier in relief I had avoided getting severely beaten up.

I knew what would have happened if I did otherwise. Not worth both of us getting hurt and losing our stuff. Giles had nothing worth stealing, and they would probably let him go in a few minutes once they searched his bag. Maybe a few punches in the stomach but nothing more. It would be for the best, a tactical retreat.

Giles and I had an unwritten code from years of being bullied. No point in both of us getting hurt. The other one would be there to get help and pick up the pieces. I was just following our code.

I strode around the corner and called his Mum. No answer. I re-dialled several times. I don't know why people bother having mobile phones as they never seem to answer them.

Around the corner, I leant against a brick wall, and rubbed my stomach better, and waited for Giles to be set free. I waited and waited for Giles, ready for the worst, expecting to see him hobbling around the corner any moment, looking a bit dirty and bruised but okay.

Ten minutes passed as I waited, and the thinning crowds of the students leaving school eyed me suspiciously. I thought about calling the police, but they would take too long and only make matters worse next term. I tried calling Giles' Mum again but still no answer. Somehow I needed to get help, as his release was taking too long. Maybe I had it wrong. Maybe something much worse had happened.

My imagination constructed worse scenarios, as only recently a neighbouring gang had killed a boy in a bullying incident gone too far. His body had been found on a disused railing embankment, his skull caved in by a lump of concrete. The gang involved lived ten miles from here, and the O'Keefes had made remarks about it to the kids at school, telling students they would be next. Probably an attempt to scare us, but they liked notoriety and for once had been outdone by another gang.

Giles and I worried such incidents could spiral out of control and that it had put ideas into the O'Keefes' minds. Remembering that incident, I couldn't help but picture Giles instead of the murdered boy, lying face up covered in blood with the top of his head brutally smashed off, and his brown eyes staring vacantly into the sky.

I didn't have any significant foresight into the workings of the O'Keefes. If I had any brilliant insights, I could have avoided them more often. The O'Keefes often acted unpredictably and maybe murder filled their minds.

The cold seeped through my coat, numbing my senses but not my continued concern for Giles. I didn't want to be standing around doing nothing but waiting in fear of what I might find. I knew a route around the

The Birth of Vengeance

alleyways into the back end of school. It would take me about five minutes, and it would get my mind off the waiting and worrying. I daren't look around the corner after Liam's warning.

As I sprinted, slipped, and skidded on the ice, the games dug into my back, a cruel reminder of the catalyst behind the incident. I stayed on my feet, bouncing off fences and walls of the paths and alleyways. Then, I threaded my way through the last of the student stragglers, breath freezing before me and body heating up from the exertion. They gawked at me, wondering why someone would run back to school on the last day of term.

Finally, my phone rang, Giles' Mum, Linda.

"Who is this?" she asked.

"It's Jonathan Harper. I'm Giles' friend," I said, slowing to a brisk walk to talk.

"What's the matter, Jonathan? Is everything okay?"

"It's Giles. A local gang has grabbed hold of him at the front gates. There was nothing I could do," I said, trying to excuse myself from any blame.

"Okay, get a teacher. I will be there as soon as possible."

I arrived at the back gate just as Mr Johnson started closing up. Mr Johnson was the caretaker and an ex-marine. He was a broad man with a hard face and shaven head. He had come out to the front gates only a few weeks ago when the gang were waiting for a victim, and he had stared them down even though outnumbered. The gang wouldn't try anything if he came out. We could still rescue Giles.

"We're shutting," he stated, pushing the gate to a close and started wrapping the chain around it and the post.

"I need help, Mr Johnson, the O'Keefe gang has kidnapped my friend," I said, as I hung onto the gate trying to get my breath back. I couldn't remember running as far before.

"Where?" he said and frowned.

"The front gate."

He unwound the chain and gestured me through, and then wound it back again and padlocked it.

"Okay, let's go, try and keep up."

He sprinted through the school, keys jangling on his belt, and I tried my best to keep up, but my tired legs couldn't maintain the pace. We ran through the empty school playgrounds and buildings, and out through the car park along the road snaking by the side of the courtyard to the front gates. I jogged around the corner into the front courtyard, and Mr Johnson stood at the front gates looking for Giles. I put in another burst and ran up to the gates, with heavy legs and a sore back from the rucksack. Just then, Linda's small blue Nissan Micra skidded to a halt a few yards away and she jumped out.

"Where is he?" she shouted, her face compressed in anguish.

"I don't know. I guess they have gone," I said.

Mr Johnson looked at the roads while shielding his eyes from the lowering sun. "I know some of their hangouts."

She waved us over. "I'll drive."

We jumped into the car and spun off down the road. I sat in the back, dumping my rucksack on the child seat next to me. Sweat poured off my forehead, but I gladly welcomed the rest as I couldn't run anymore.

We dived down the back roads and crisscrossed the main routes away from the school. Mr Johnson directed us and scouted for a sign of the gang. Linda's head scanned left and right, frantically looking for any sign of her son. Other students walked and cycled back in groups and by themselves, but no gang or Giles. We continued skidding around the corners, with the pine tree air freshener swinging and spinning about off the mirror inside. I felt sick in the back of her car from the sharp turns and frantic looking from side-to-side out of the windows.

We headed further into the estate and into the gang's territory, and we saw fewer students from my school as the houses got smaller and more broken down, and the main block of flats up ahead loomed closer.

We found him after half an hour, walking along the pavement with the gang encircling him and shoving him along.

"Over there," I shouted, pointing over Linda's shoulder to the gang.

She looked over at them, judging the situation, and drove further down the road. She hammered the brakes on, and I jerked forwards and jarred into my seatbelt. The car reversed and then crunched into first gear. The wheels spun as the tyres screeched with smoke spiralling up into the air, and we drove back towards the gang. I swallowed back my sick.

They noticed the car, but sights of erratic driving were common in this estate, so the gang paid little attention. We swerved off the road, bounced up the pavement, and headed straight at the gang. Linda slammed on the brakes, but the car's wheels locked up.

I braced myself as we skidded towards the group. The first member of the gang, Liam, tried to put his hands out to halt the car, but the bonnet smashed his legs from under him and catapulted him into the air. His body spun around and travelled onto the windscreen, cracking it into a web. Liam bounced up the car, banging off the top of the roof and landing in a twisted pile.

The car clipped Patrick, and he spun around, hitting his head on the road. Some of the gang laid scattered about, as they had knocked each other over to escape. The ones at the back ran as soon as the car piled into them. Somehow, Giles avoided the car and stood in the middle of the mayhem unscathed, with gang members spread about him and running off.

The car whipped us forwards and backwards in our seats, and my head and neck seized in agony. Linda jumped out of the car, rushed over to Giles, but slipped on the ice and nearly knocked him over.

"Stay in the car," Mr Johnson shouted into the back seat while opening the door.

He jumped out of the car and ran around to the twisted body of Liam on the pavement behind us. Mr Johnson whipped his phone out and dialled as he knelt down. My head and neck hurt from the whiplash, and I had gone into shock from the collision. My sick clawed its way back, and I couldn't stop it. I opened the door and emptied my lunch onto the road next to the head of Patrick O'Keefe. Lumps of half-digested chips and sausage splattered into his hair.

I spat the last of the sick out as Patrick regained consciousness. In front, Giles hugged his Mum. Behind, Mr Johnson spoke with the emergency services. I wanted to get away from this disaster. I didn't want any part of this accident.

I grabbed my rucksack, scrambled out of the car, and ran away from the accident. Away from any involvement. Away from any responsibility.

"Jonathan, come back," Linda shouted, but I didn't stop. I didn't even look back.

CHAPTER TWO

After the accident, everything became a bit of a blur. I didn't know the area well, as this wasn't a place I had ever walked about or wanted to walk around. I ran back towards school, hoping I would recognise the roads back home.

In the distance, I saw a chip shop sign, a blue jumping fish on a white background, "Chip Away." We sometimes went there for food on the way home. I'd never been so pleased to see that sign in my life.

I cut across the road and picked my way through a few back streets that connected back to my usual route. Up ahead, I could make out the local newsagents. I was on the way home and away from the tangled mess I had left behind on the estate. Even though I was in an area of safety, I kept running all the way. I wanted to put as much distance as possible between that accident and me. The O'Keefes wouldn't let this go unanswered. There would be consequences.

I rushed inside, slammed the door, slung my rucksack down the hallway, and raced straight upstairs to my bedroom. The house lay empty, as just Dad and I lived there. I lay on my bed in the dark, retracing my steps and trying to make sense of what had just happened. The way the car had hit those gang members; I knew it was serious.

I took deep breaths to recover from the long run back, and I realised I needed to let my Dad know what had happened. I took my coat off, walked downstairs, and swiped the cordless phone off the side as I walked into the kitchen.

The filthy kitchen floor stuck to my feet and squeaked. The dirty dishes from the day before yesterday's meal still sat on the kitchen side, ready to be loaded into the dishwasher.

I phoned my Dad's office number. It rang for some time, as it always did.

"Hello."

"Hi Dad, it's me."

"Why are you calling? I am in the middle of an important experiment."

"I know, I'm sorry, but the O'Keefe gang kidnapped Giles. I got help from the caretaker and Giles' Mum. But she drove into them on the rough estate and knocked a few of them over. I think some of them may be seriously hurt."

"Are you okay?"

"Yes. I am fine, but I didn't hang about. I ran off and came straight home."

"As long as you are okay, it doesn't matter. Probably best not to get caught up with that gang. They already target you."

"I know, ever since I started at that school. Just seven more months and I can be free of them."

"Yes. Then you can leave that awful school. Order yourself a pizza and get an early night. I will speak to Giles' family tomorrow."

"Okay, Dad."

"Good. Now I have to get back to my experiment, it is at a critical point. Bye." The phone hung up. It was a typical conversation with my Dad when he was working.

I dialled straight away to the local pizza delivery, ordered a pepperoni pizza and watched a couple of forgettable films before crashing out on the sofa, exhausted and scared. Scared of what had happened and afraid of what might happen next.

#

The next morning, daylight peered through the sides of the curtains, waking me up. My legs felt sore, neck ached, and my head pounded. I stretched out on the sofa, squeezing my legs out, receiving pain and pleasure as my muscles extended.

I woke up and pulled off the blanket that covered me. I guessed my Dad threw it over me when he came in last night. The TV had been turned off, and the pizza box lay on the floor with a few slices left. I sat up and ate the cold pizza and switched on the TV. I flicked through the channels to find something to watch while I ate my leftover pizza and thought about what had happened yesterday. After eating, I pulled the curtains, and the daylight streamed through, highlighting the dust as it blew back across the floor.

The house, as usual, looked a mess with old cups of tea and coffee sat on the tables next to the sofa. The air smelt musty, as the windows hadn't been opened and carpet not hoovered since my aunty came around four months ago. I shuffled into the kitchen, still waking up and rubbing my sore neck from the accident. The white kitchen floor stuck to my feet and my shoes made the familiar squeaky sound. Inside, the dirty dishes were still piled high on the kitchen side. I washed up a cup and made a cup of tea. I cleaned the dirty dishes away and tidied away the mess while taking warm slugs of tea as I went.

I trudged upstairs and into the shower room to freshen up. I brushed my teeth and looked at myself in the plastic cabinet mirrors. Was this really my life? My blue eyes were tinged with blood and lack of sleep was marked by dark circles underneath. I flattened down my dark slept-on hair. I didn't sleep well on the sofa but couldn't be bothered to get changed and go to bed properly.

I finished brushing and swilled out. I stared back into the mirror again and flashed back to the accident, Liam smashing onto the car. Once I left school, I always hoped that life would get better. I only had to survive seven more months, but that now seemed impossible. In seven more months, I would have finished my last exams, and I planned to do my A-levels at a local further education college instead of the school's sixth form. I wanted to get away from that place and those people as soon as possible.

I couldn't help but think what my Mum would have said to me if she were alive. I had spent nine months with her in her womb. She had already died by the time I was born; she didn't get the chance to hold me for a single second. Through my life, I often thought of Mum when times got hard and would try to picture her and imagine what she would say. I had also kept her name, Harper. In the hospital, they put me down as Baby Harper on the forms purely for admin purposes. Dad never corrected the mistake. I guessed it helped him remember her, proof of her sacrifice.

I stripped off, got in the shower, and allowed the hot water to wash not just the dirt away but also my thoughts and feelings. I grabbed a towel and went into my room to dry and dress. I sorted through my least dirty clothes and put on a pair of jeans and a t-shirt before walking downstairs with armfuls of washing.

Dad's bed squeaked as he got up, and his footsteps dragged across the carpet and the bedroom door opened. He thumped down the stairs and wandered through to the kitchen, with his dressing gown hanging off his small pale frame. The hours he worked at night and lack of daylight showed; his skin pale and tired. He usually wore little round glasses, but he could cope without for a while. According to the predicted charts, I would follow his build, and I reckoned I would inherit his hairline. He had lost his hair on top but had unkempt fluffy bits at the sides.

He sat and ate breakfast at the kitchen table after he had cleared a space from old newspapers and comics. I explained in more detail what had happened the day before with the gang grabbing Giles, the car accident, and my running away.

"Don't worry about running off. As I said last night, I will give Giles' Dad a call later. Best not to get involved in these types of things," he said, munching on his cornflakes as he glanced up from an old newspaper.

The Birth of Vengeance

Later on, after he spoke with Giles' Dad, he switched off the TV in the living room, and sat on the sofa opposite ready to talk. I turned to face him, prepared for the news.

"Giles' Mum was arrested for dangerous driving, and they are pursuing a case of kidnapping against the O'Keefes as well," he said.

A small smile broke across my face on hearing the O'Keefes would not get away with it.

"Is Giles okay?" I asked.

"He is fine but the boy his Mum hit, Liam, is in the hospital still. They doubt he will walk again," he said and pursed his lips together.

I knew it was going to be bad as soon as I saw him motionless on the ground after he bounced over the roof. Again, I couldn't contain a smile. Revenge at last even if it was an accident. However, my pleasure at his paralysis quickly turned to worry. It would mean consequences for Giles and me, as the O'Keefes weren't a forgiving family. They would be hell-bent on revenge for Liam's accident and angry about the kidnapping charges. I started to sweat. Things were going to get messy.

"Liam is part of that gang. They will come after us," I said.

"Probably, but they don't realise you are involved. Good thing you ran away. It will be best if you don't see Giles for a while."

Maybe he was right. Maybe I would be okay, but I needed to speak with Giles and redeem myself for walking away at the front gates. "I can't just abandon him now. We have been friends for years."

"I know, but this is your exam year. You can't afford to get involved, and we need to keep you out of sight."

"Why?"

"You will be a key witness in the trial against the O'Keefes. If they are found guilty, it should go a long way to clearing Linda's name of dangerous driving. I have told Giles' Dad that there will be no contact from now on until things settle down. This includes at school. It's best for everyone. It will help save Linda."

"You can't do this."

"I can and I have. This isn't up for debate. It's only you and me, and I can't be around to watch out for you during the day if they come after you," he said, raising his voice and standing up.

I stomped upstairs and put some music on to drown him out. Yet again, everything came down to him. However, he couldn't stop me from contacting Giles. I decided to email him, but the computer wouldn't connect.

"I have disconnected your Internet connection," Dad shouted up the stairs, "and I have taken your phone."

I went to the top of the stairs. "I can't abandon him. He will need friends."

"It is not our concern. The teachers have promised to keep a special eye on him. You must stay away from him. It is best for everyone in the long run. I promised your Mum I would protect you and this is your last year of school. Your grades are all that matters."

I couldn't speak to Giles, and I had no other friends. I spent the rest of the week stuck inside the house, and I only left once to give my statement at the police station. The rest of the time, I played on my computer, listened to music, and even studied for something to do. Anything had to be better than sitting around and reliving the car crash. But the memories lingered on of Liam bouncing over the bonnet of the car, smashing the windscreen, and Patrick lying on the ground next to my pool of sick.. I worried about what would happen on returning to school. At least studying distracted me from my pending problems.

#

After the holiday, I went back to school, and I came into class late and signed in. Chaos reigned as usual. Students threw paper balls about, and their phones beeped and rang. Some shouted across the room, while others sat quietly in the corners huddled together, keeping out of the way and holding private conversations. I overhead students discussing what had happened with Giles and the O'Keefes. While talking, they glanced over to the corner of the room at Giles sat by himself and Patrick and his friend Dave sat behind him. I guessed everyone knew.

The teacher, Mr May, seemed none the wiser about the situation, even though the headmaster said they would keep an eye out. He did, as he usually did, and read his newspaper, waiting for the bell to signal his first lesson.

Patrick and Dave whispered to Giles, but I couldn't hear what they said above the noise. I guessed from the contorted features as they spoke that it wasn't pleasant. Giles' face crumbled, and his shoulders hunched in to protect himself from their vicious words.

Then Giles spotted me signing in at Mr May's desk. He looked relieved, but his face scrunched up in anger as yet again I walked away. Patrick laughed and pointed at me. I withdrew to the door, red-faced from the attention and ashamed I had deserted Giles again.

The bell rang. I bolted straight out of the door, marching to my first lesson and away from Giles and the extra attention. I sat in the next classroom, hoping someone else would sit next to me before Giles arrived,

The Birth of Vengeance

but the class filled up and everyone sat at desks around me, but no one next to me. Giles would arrive soon and I would have no choice. Maybe it was for the best. I decided I would explain everything to him when he arrived. However, the lesson started and he never came, nor did Patrick and Dave. It boded ill that all three of them hadn't made it to the next lesson.

I wondered what had happened to Giles, wishing I had gone and sat next to him at registration regardless of what Dad said, and the evil looks Patrick and Dave gave me. We were supposed to be best friends, and Giles would have tried to take care of me. He always had done.

I darted out as soon as the lesson ended, hoping to find him and redeem myself. I tried the chess room first as we sometimes dropped in to arrange games for lunchtime and to hide away during breaks. I opened the door but couldn't see Giles. The rest of the club, from the years below us, had already arrived. They were the closest people I could call friends after Giles.

"Giles been in?" I asked.

I received a stream of shaking heads. I walked past the cloakroom area and dived inside the curtain of coats hanging up. The cloakroom carved an alcove in the wall, and we would sometimes hide behind the coats out of the way. No luck here either.

I didn't have much time left before the next bell and rushed on to the art room. Again, I got a shake of the head. I slouched off to my next lesson, hoping I would find him on the way. I wanted to apologise for ignoring him earlier in registration and explain to him why I hadn't been in touch and tell him I would do the right thing in court.

I shuffled into the room and saw Giles sitting at the front already. A moment of relief stood me up straight until I realised Patrick and Dave sat behind him. Giles' clothes appeared dishevelled, and his cheeks bruised and face stained with tears. Patrick and Dave stared at me as I walked in. Dave ran his fingers across his throat and pointed at me. I looked away and marched to the back of the class, doing as my Dad instructed. Giles' face streamed with tears as I walked away, leaving him to the bullies.

My resolve had melted away, and I had to face the truth that I was a coward. When it came to the crunch, I ran off and hid away, hoping I would be left in peace. That was what I had always done to cope with the bullying. Even though my best friend needed me, I still couldn't find the guts to stand by his side.

Ashamed and feeling guilty, I sat at the back of the classroom hiding from everyone's gaze, unable to look anyone in the eye. Tears burned my eyes, and I shielded them behind my hands and pretended to read. The other students whispered and glanced around at me and then back at Giles. I couldn't believe the teachers had let them get away with it during school hours. Obviously, Mr May had done nothing to ensure Giles' safety, just as he hadn't at the school gates on the day of the kidnapping. I hated him.

Over the course of the next week, they inflicted new tortures upon Giles and gave me new reasons to avoid him. The gang subjected him to the old-fashioned head in the toilet, stealing his clothes, general beatings, taking his money, and wrecking his books. During that week, I heard of even worse events that I hoped were not true but just teenage kids over-exaggerating. Those who hung around him were caught up in the events and either got the same treatment or made to take part.

In the end, no one would even sit with him in class or eat lunch with him at dinner times. Giles never walked home anymore. At home, cyber bullying continued on the day's events, with text messages and posts on social network sites. I heard through the other kids at school that his older sister had been attacked by the O'Keefe sisters while on a night out. The O'Keefes hounded Giles' family day and night, with physical assaults, prank phone calls, and house and car windows smashed.

On the Friday of the first week back, I dipped out of maths to go to the toilet, but the sound of sobbing in the corner of the cloakroom stopped me in my tracks. On the floor, I spotted a green rucksack. I scouted around before approaching.

"Giles, is that you? Are you okay?"

He shifted out from behind the coats and lifted his head up. The tears rolled down his freshly bruised face, eyes stinging red and nose dripping wet. He sucked back the tears and wiped his eyes with the sleeve of his blazer.

Giles took a moment to focus. His eyes narrowed and forehead glowed red with rage. He jumped out of his seat, charged, and shoulder barged me straight in the chest, forcing the wind from my lungs as I hit the hard concrete floor. As I rolled over, he punched me in the back, and I twisted around and shoved him away.

He shouted, with fists raging and the tears sprinkling off his face. "This is your fault. Why did you abandon me that day? Why did you wind up my Mum so much? Why did you stop being my friend?"

He stared at me, waiting for an answer, but I had no reasonable answer and just stared mouth wide open, hoping words would tumble out of their own accord. He slumped and then stumbled away down the corridor, wiping his nose on the sleeve of his blazer as he turned the corner. The sound of his snuffling echoed back down the empty hallway to remind me of my guilt.

Our friendship was finished. How could I ever apologise and make things right? I had abandoned him. I had lost my best and only friend.

CHAPTER THREE

The memory of Giles in floods of tears flashed across my mind every few minutes, pricking my conscience with guilt and embarrassment at deserting him. If only I had refused to walk away from the gates. I would have probably got a beating and lost my games, but that would have been better than losing my best friend.

My fury rose against all those other people who watched on and did nothing to help. The teachers and parents who turned a blind eye outside the front of the school. All too busy or too scared to get involved. If just one of them had come across, then others may have helped them, but no one cared if a couple of young boys got beaten up. It was an everyday occurrence far as they were concerned. All part of growing up. They could have helped, but they didn't, and they have no idea how much damage their inaction caused. Instead, they left a couple of scared and bullied kids to fend for themselves.

Home alone at night again, I had nearly dulled the memory and the anger with a few films and curry ready meal. It approached 11 pm, and I cleared away the empty plate, turned off the TV, and went to bed.

After a while, I drifted off to painful flashbacks of Giles crying when the sound of smashing glass snapped me out of my sleep. I bolted out of bed and ran onto the landing, slapping the light on and forcing my eyes to squint. I bashed open the door to the spare room at the front of the house and clambered over the half-filled cardboard boxes with scientific textbooks, and I briefly pondered why my Dad had been packing before I pressed my face to the window. A couple of kids in hoodies sprinted off down the street. I recognised the hooded tops and the way they ran. It looked like the O'Keefe brothers.

I clambered back over the boxes and thundered downstairs to check the house. I pushed open the door to the living room to get sight of them out of the window. I hit the lights inside the door as I entered, and then pain stabbed at the soles of my feet. I jumped back out the door again. Glass lay scattered across the living room floor, covering the carpet and sofa, and a brick sat in the middle of the floor in an admission of guilt. The curtains flapped from the wind blowing through a jagged hole in the glass that had knocked over the picture frames on the windowsill. My favourite picture of my Mum, when she was heavily pregnant, had smashed to the floor. The only picture I had of us together.

I hopped backwards, swearing and hobbling into the kitchen while leaving bloody footprints down the hallway. I grabbed the phone as I limped into the kitchen and crashed into a seat, and then called my Dad.

As per usual, the phone rang for ages. "Hello."

"Hi Dad, it's me. Sorry to disturb you, but someone has thrown a brick through the living room window."

"Okay. Call the police and I will come home. I just need five minutes to handover. Stay inside. Don't do anything stupid. Bye."

I phoned the police, then pulled the first aid kit out of the cupboard, bandaged my foot, and hobbled up the stairs to get dressed.

I put on a pair of jeans and a t-shirt, and then pulled my sock over the bandage. I lay on my bed, waiting for someone to arrive, not wanting to go back downstairs on my own. After about twenty minutes, I heard muffled voices outside and car doors clunked shut. I walked back downstairs, trying to keep my weight off my injured foot. I opened the front door, which had "Grass," sprayed on it in wet red paint. I touched it with my fingertips and then wiped it absent mindedly across my jeans, smearing red stripes down the sides.

Outside in the dark winter's night, Dad stood next to a policewoman who took notes as they exchanged words. The radio in her car crackled and muffled voices echoed in the empty vehicle. Her colleague, a man, walked down the path to the next-door neighbour's house and spoke into his radio as he went. The blue lights of the police car were flashing and reflecting off the windows of nearby houses, filling the street with its taint. The curtains of neighbours twitched, and they peered out observing the spectacle.

Dad pointed towards the front door where I stood, and then walked down the pathway and ushered me back inside. He scanned the broken window and the red letters across the door. He stepped inside, opened the living room door, and took in the destruction. He sucked in a deep breath and mumbled as he exhaled.

"The police will be here in a minute to examine the scene. Let's go into the kitchen and have a cuppa," he said, shutting the door.

"What happened to you?" he said, as I limped on in front of him.

"I stood on the glass and cut my foot open. It's okay, I bandaged it."

I pulled out a chair and lowered myself in, and Dad leant against the doorframe.

"I guess the gang has found you. They must know you are a witness in both cases," he said matter-of-factly with his arms crossed.

I had already guessed that. The brick was just the start.

"I can't go back to school, they will kill me."

Dad nodded. "You're right. I will try to sort something out."

His agreement surprised me. I felt I had been saved, else I would be the next victim for Patrick and Dave if I returned to school. His face then took a more severe turn.

"I heard this evening from Giles' Dad. Giles tried to commit suicide this evening. He slit his wrists in the bath. He is alive but has been admitted to a psychiatric hospital."

I recoiled from the news. I didn't want to believe it after Giles had attacked me. Had seeing me been the last straw; the thing that pushed him over the edge? I didn't know for sure, but it felt like it. The tears welled up in my eyes, and I wiped them away with the edge of my hand.

"It's my fault. If only I hadn't ignored him. If only I had refused to walk away from those gates and stood by his side," I said.

"It's not your fault. There is no way you could have stopped a whole gang by yourself. It's the school's fault. They should have looked after him. They should have looked after both of you. They promised."

It now made sense why he agreed so quickly for me to stay out of school. It would have been me next if I had returned. He could've found me lying in the bath with my wrists slit, hoping it would be the end to the suffering. Giles had always been the stronger of the two of us; there was no way I would cope.

The policewoman tapped on the door and walked in.

"Hi, I need to examine the scene, then take a statement," she said.

"Okay, help yourself," Dad replied and pointed to the living room door.

She came back out in a few minutes with the brick in a clear bag and walked into the kitchen.

"Going to need a statement, as well. I hear you are giving evidence against the O'Keefe gang. You are very brave," she said and placed the brick in the centre of the table.

I didn't feel brave, and her words solidified my growing fear. She took the statement and kept going on about the O'Keefes, saying it was time someone stood up to them. She told us stories of how others had changed their minds, and this wasn't the first time they tried to harass the witnesses. It wasn't encouraging. I wanted to tell her to shut up as if things weren't serious enough without her acting as their PR. She finally finished and wished us good luck, as we would need it, apparently. Dad walked her outside and locked the door.

"You go back to sleep, Jon. I am going to tidy up and work out what to do next," Dad said. I didn't argue and went back to bed from where I

The Birth of Vengeance

listened to the noises downstairs of the vacuum.

I went through a rollercoaster of emotions: scared, relieved and guilty. Scared that the O'Keefe gang had targeted me and to giving evidence against them at the trial, but relieved I didn't have to face them at school again. I wouldn't have to go through the hell Giles went through. Then I felt guilty about Giles' suicide attempt. My heart said it was my fault, but my head said otherwise. The school, the police and parents could have all stopped this from happening on that fateful day at the front gates. They could have all made more of an effort in the aftermath of the accident to protect us from the gang. They all knew what would happen next, but all seemed unwilling to prevent it as all too scared of the O'Keefe gang.

I tried to sleep, but I kept waking up through the night at the slightest sound, scared they had returned, but it was just Dad tidying up.

I slept in late, having only fallen asleep in the early hours of the morning. Downstairs, I heard Dad walking about, still awake from last night. I lay in bed and thought about how we could get out of this problem, but it was no good. My world was ending. I would have to stand up in court to give evidence against the O'Keefes. This wouldn't end easily. The O'Keefes wouldn't let it. I would spend the rest of my life living in fear that they would come after me for revenge. I could never stop them, as I would never be strong enough.

The time hit 11:47 am and I slid out of bed, wrapped my dressing gown on, and wandered downstairs. Music filled the kitchen as Dad whistled along to folk music from the radio and accompanied it with the clattering of cutlery as he tidied away.

I opened the living room door. The floor had been swept clean of glass, and the broken window covered with wood. The rest of the room had been cleaned and dusted, with the dirty old mugs finally removed. The picture of Mum sat back on the windowsill minus the broken glass. Surprised by the cleanliness, I shut the door and shuffled into the kitchen for breakfast. The bloody footprints in the hallway had been washed away, and the kitchen floor washed clean, removing the familiar squeak of my slippers.

"Morning, sleep okay?" Dad asked cheerfully, smiling as I entered the room.

"Eventually," I said, looking at him side-on.

"You fancy a cooked breakfast, son?" he asked.

"Yes ... er please."

Dad oiled the pan and turned on the gas. Orange juice and a pot of coffee sat on the table, and I poured myself a cup of each.

"I've good news," he said.

"I guessed," I said, and took a gulp of coffee to wake up, trying to prepare myself for what could be classed as good news.

"I called work this morning to tell them what had happened, and I would need time off," he said, as he dropped the sausages into the sizzling pan. "They made us an offer. I think you will like it."

"Okay," I replied, unsure what it could be. How could my Dad's work possibly help?

"They have a house we can move into temporarily. Plus, they will get a tutor for your home study as long as I keep working," he said.

"Why?" I asked. It all seemed too good to be true; there must be a catch.

"When your exams are finished, they want us to move to London for a new job. My research is critical, apparently. They can't afford to have me away from work."

I sat in stunned silence, trying to understand. I drank more coffee, trying to wake up and process the information. How could Dad's work carry that much importance? I never really thought about it before, and I knew not to ask as he worked for the government. It sounded like a perfect solution, protection from the gang and a move to the other end of the country where they would never find us.

"So what do you think?" he asked, as he threw the mushrooms into the frying pan.

"New life and safety, or stay here in fear? There is no choice. Anything is better than this. Let's do it."

"Good, I thought you would say yes. Let's eat up and then pack. We can move in today, as they will send someone around to help us."

"Excellent," I replied, and poured the rest of the coffee into my mouth.

I sat in a surreal daze. I had woken up in complete despair of what would happen next, but Dad's work had come to the rescue, and all we had to do was move to London. Leeds had nothing for us anyway. I had lost my best friend and Dad's work was the only thing important to him. Finally, something good had happened, and I would get as far away from the O'Keefe gang as possible. The solution seemed perfect. Almost too good to be true.

CHAPTER FOUR

My first day at my new college and my first year of A-level studies commenced. I had somehow passed my exams and could carry on into further education. The time hiding away and home study had helped, as there was nowhere else to go or anything else to do. Studying helped take my mind off my problems and helped me forget. In maths and physics, the answer is right or wrong; working to fix problems gave me something to focus upon and gave me control over my life. I refused to let the O'Keefes win and passing my exams felt like the only way I could fight back before the trial.

The temporary house was in amongst the barracks on an army base. Also, the location of the research centre where my Dad worked. Inside the barbed wire and surrounded by armed guards, the gang could never reach me. The tutor, Joanna, the base commander's wife, had guided me through my studies and even taken me to my exams.

During this time, I discovered the real world without the constrained ideas of teachers and authority. Joanna had given me a leather jacket and other clothes from the army lost property. In the jacket pocket, I discovered an iPod, and I plugged it into my stereo. The speakers blasted out intense and dark thrash metal, goth and rap music. The music and lyrics shared my life experiences. I understood the lyrics and what they meant. Even though I had never been to an American high school or grown up in a trailer park. Being a teenager was the same everywhere.

I changed hiding away from school. I grew my hair long. It had never been allowed as the school had a strict hair length policy. I dressed differently and changed my image to wear lots of black and grunge clothing, but I also became a recluse. I rarely left the compound. On occasions, I walked around to the local corner shop, five minutes outside, to buy magazines and snacks. The whole time out of the army base, I remained on guard for the first sign of trouble, knowing a short dash back to the army gates would ensure sanctuary. I felt safest inside the fences, listening to my new music and studying.

The inevitable move to London came as a shock, as I didn't know where to go or where to avoid in the new location. I stayed at home, not wishing to venture out in case I walked into the wrong neighbourhood or crossed the wrong people. Eventually, I would need to leave the house for my first day of college and that day had arrived.

I walked along with the headmaster to the sixth form college, ready to start afresh. A new place, new people, and I decided it would be a new me as well. I chose not to discuss with anyone what happened in Leeds. I had deleted all my social media accounts, so I couldn't be traced. I didn't want everyone thinking that I grassed, or I suffered from bullying. I didn't want to be targeted again. I wanted a new life, a chance to leave the old fears behind and start anew. I didn't want to be scared anymore. I wanted to sleep at night without worrying about glass shattering or being attacked. I wanted to walk around during the day without fear of being beaten up and mugged.

The first day of college was going to be the first day of my new life. No one had any pre-conceived ideas. I could reinvent myself and be a brand new person. First impressions lasted, so that day had to go well.

The headmaster strode down the hallways, with the smell of strong coffee puffing out before him. Students parted the ways as we marched towards the sixth form college. The college continued from the state school, "St Luker's", and most of the students had come straight from the school and into the sixth form college to do A-Levels.

"Don't know why you're so special that I have to take you," he said as we walked.

"I don't know," I said, unaware of any special arrangements.

"I have lots to do. It's the first day of term," he said. He stopped and pointed at a boy who had just pushed a girl over.

"Boy, go and stand outside my room and wait for me," he shouted.

The boy trudged off, and the other students laughed at him. The girl's friends helped her up and shoved him as he walked past and flung insults at him.

"That's enough, I will deal with it," the headmaster said.

"Come on, Harper, don't stop," he said and walked off again down the hallway.

We entered the sixth form common room to the noise of my new classmates, some seated on black sofas and chairs posted around square desks. Most of them chatting and discussing the summer's events and what classes they had enrolled in this year. I guessed they knew each other from being at school together at St Luker's in the previous year, or in their second year of the sixth form.

A few students searched through the bookshelves against the walls looking for free textbooks. The rest of the walls carried motivational posters like "Challenge" and "Success," of people climbing to the top of mountains with some pop psychology statement underneath. Someone had

The Birth of Vengeance

stuck a fake de-motivational poster under it, "Failure," of someone falling off the same mountain. A few more students busied themselves at the far end in the kitchen area, cutting up toast and pouring hot water into cups to make tea and coffee.

The students were all dressed in their best clothes, trying on their first day at college to make a positive impression on the others in the class. Their new designer clothes were neatly ironed, and I imagined had been bought by their mothers only days before. How sad and shallow.

I'd taken another route. I had dressed in my darkest and blackest clothes, trying desperately to send a different message. I wasn't trying to make friends or impress people. I wanted people to leave me alone and think I could fight. So, I wore frayed and cut denim jeans, black army boots, and an old roughed up black leather jacket. Underneath, I wore an old black t-shirt with, "Motorhead," written across it in silver letters.

I scanned the room, looking at the attractive girls and noting gangs of boys to avoid when one girl caught my attention. Her hair shone flame dark red, and she sat quietly next to a goth girl with short dark bobbed hair. They sat over the far side of the room on a black sofa under the window. She stood out in the room in contrast to the other clones of dyed blonde girls who were all plastered in makeup.

She had attracted the attention of several other admirers, a group of guys sitting at the table next to where I stood with the headmaster. They peered over and then whispered to one another. A few of the girls in the class looked over at her; their noses wrinkled in disgust and contempt, and then they spitefully whispered to one another. They seemed unhappy that she had attracted the attention of the men in the room.

She appeared older than the rest of the students in the common room. Her figure seemed more mature, and her face gave the appearance of being more experienced. Her womanly figure only contributed to the attention she received, as her bright fashionable clothes accentuated her figure, working in tandem with her long wavy red hair flowing down her shoulders and onto her chest. She was impossible not to notice. She must have been aware of the effect she had on all the men in the room. Yet, she sat there curling her hair in between her fingers, checking her nails and then talking with her friend. She seemed to be utterly oblivious to the admiring glances and the disgusting glares, either that or she didn't care.

I felt attracted to her immediately, and I knew straight away that she would be way out of my league. I would be lucky even to get to talk to her. The stark reality of the situation made my shoulders sink with feelings of hopelessness, and I tried to focus on getting on with the school year. Even the headmaster stopped and stared at her for a while, rubbing his unkempt white beard, before he remembered his position and clapped his hands together.

"Hi, everyone, this is Jonathan Harper. Please make him feel welcome," he quickly announced, then said hello to the teacher, Miss Goodwin. He looked over at the flamed haired girl once more, shook his head, sighed, and then strode out of the room.

Miss Goodwin smiled, and I guessed she couldn't have been that long out of university.

"Hello, Jonathan. I have arranged some guides for you today."

Everyone had gone back to his or her conversation after glancing over at the brief introduction. I saw no sign of the unlucky person who would act as my guide. Miss Goodwin placed her hand on my arm and took me over to the far side of the room directly in front of the flamed haired girl.

"Jonathan, this is Scarlett," she said, showing her hand towards the flamed haired girl, "this is Mary," she added, pointing to her friend. "I have asked them to look after you and show you about. They both only started this year as well, but both made it to the orientation day."

I staggered back a step. I couldn't believe after everything I had just thought and felt about her, that I had received an introduction to this gorgeous woman. My excitement returned. My heart pounded in my chest and a glow of nervous perspiration seeped across my body. Now next to Scarlett, I saw her face up close and felt drawn into her large green eyes. Her skin was fresh, lips full, and her nose daintily sat between high cheekbones.

Scarlett nodded in acceptance and offered a weak smile.

"Hi, sit down," Mary said, motioning toward the stool in front of her and smiling.

Mary wore black-rimmed glasses and gothic clothes. She had a few piercings in her ears and one through her nose. She looked younger than Scarlett did, and I guessed nearer to my age, having come straight from GCSE's.

I dived onto the seat, wanting to blend in as soon as possible. The guys in the room watched me jealously as I sat down. Scarlett just continued playing with her nails and twirling her hair around her fingers. No reaction to my presence beyond that first nod hello.

"Where you from Jonathan?" Mary asked.

"Leeds."

"Leeds!" Scarlett blurted out and spun around, letting go of her hair and it twirling away onto her shoulders. A smile beamed across her face, and her eyes lit up. Her accent, the same as mine, gave away her sudden excitement.

"Yeah," I replied and smiled.

I had a way in. She wanted to talk to me now.

"Whereabouts?"

"I went to St Teresa's school, next to the Meanwood council estate."

"You lived in Meanwood?" she said and shifted back.

"No. The school was next to it. I lived on the other side, in Beckshill."

"Sorry. I heard of problems with the kids from Meanwood. I went to school over the other side at St Mary's academy."

"I heard someone from your school got killed by a gang?" I said.

"It was a horrible business. A gang from another estate, Holdforths, followed a kid home from school and dragged him down the embankment. I think they just wanted to steal his money and phone, but the boy slipped and smashed his skull open."

"Is that what happened? We heard they had hit him over the head with a rock."

"No. The story got out of control. But I heard someone from your school got kidnapped by a gang. We heard they wanted to kill him to prove they were as hard as the Holdforths' estate gang."

I swallowed hard. I didn't want to let on how much I knew. "It's true. But he got away."

"We heard about it. His Mum drove over the gang and seriously injured one of them. But the kid tried to commit suicide later on from the bullying."

"He did, but he survived. Hopefully, the O'Keefe gang will go to prison for trying to kidnap him."

"You know of the gang?"

I paused for a moment. Had I said too much? "Everyone at our school knew of the O'Keefe gang."

"Of course. Everyone knows of their local gang. I am glad to be away from them."

I nodded. "And me. No gangs here, I hope?"

She shook her head. "Sorry. But they get everywhere. The local gang is called the Rude Crew. They hang about the front of the school most days, but there is a back way out."

"Oh. I will keep out of their way. I might use the back exit anyway as it is the quickest route home."

"So what did you get up to in Leeds?"

"We used to hang out at the cinema in the shopping mall if we could get a lift into the city centre, or just around each other's houses playing computer games," I said.

"We used to go to that cinema as well. Easiest one to drive to."

The bell rang for the first lesson.

"Catch up with you both at lunch. I have got biology and chemistry," said Mary, and picked up her bag and walked out of the room.

"Physics is our first class. I will show you the way," Scarlett said.

It surprised me she had chosen physics, didn't seem the sort of subject a girl like her would study. I would have expected something more creative like English literature.

Scarlett directed me out the door, and I walked alongside her as she led the way down the grey corridors to the first lesson.

"So how long you been in London?" she asked.

"Only moved in about five weeks ago. Wasn't sure of the results I would get, so the college choice was a bit last minute. That is why I missed the orientation day."

"I have been down here for a few months. Why did you leave Leeds?" Scarlett asked.

"My Dad got offered a new job," I said.

"What about the rest of your family? What do they do?"

"It's just my Dad and me."

"Oh," Scarlett said.

"How about you? What is your story?" I asked, trying to move off the awkward subject.

"Parents divorced and I failed A-levels first time around, so trying again now. I have moved down here with my Mum to start afresh, as she got a new job."

Scarlett walked into the classroom and grabbed a table at the front. I hesitated and looked around, trying to work out where to sit, not sure if she wanted me to sit next to her.

"I have got us some seats," Scarlett said.

I smiled, as pleased she wanted to carry on the conversation.

"Thanks," I said, sitting next to her and dumping my bag on the table.

The rest of the class ambled in and then the teacher, Miss Goodwin, behind them. The class numbered only ten people and we sat two per bench facing the teacher and whiteboard at the front.

Miss Goodwin handed out some textbooks and looked through her notes.

As I pulled out some paper and pens, my iPod slid onto the table.

"Can I have a look?" Scarlett asked.

I nodded, but worried she would hate my music.

"I love this song," she said, looking at the music currently playing.

She flicked through the rest of the iPod and commented on my other music choices.

"I've got some albums I think you would like. I will send you the playlist," she said, handing the iPod back.

I couldn't believe how much we had in common already, came from the same place, same classes, same music and I wondered what else. The class started, and Scarlett helped me out on a few equations, explaining how it worked.

The bell rang, signalling the next class.

"I think you are in maths with me as well. Shall we walk down and sit together again?" she said.

"Yeah, that would be great," I answered, almost falling over my tongue as I rushed to agree with her.

We walked down the corridor to the next class, and Scarlett walked down to the back of the room.

"Let's sit here. We can talk more at the back," she said and winked.

I nodded and walked by her side.

"So what is your favourite film?" I asked.

"Oh, I love sci-fi. It has to be Star Wars and the Matrix as my favourites. In fact, I just bought Star Wars on Blu-ray," she answered.

Things just got better.

"Really, I would love to watch them with you," I answered, pushing my luck.

Scarlett eyed me, paused for a moment, and then smiled.

"That sounds like a good idea. Yeah, maybe we could one day."

I had gotten away with it. In fact, I wanted to jump up and down with joy, as she seemed to genuinely like the idea.

We carried on talking, and I discovered she liked computer games, and we exchanged Xbox Live ID's to play against or with each other online. My luck had changed with the introduction to Scarlett, and her being asked to look after me for the day. My life in London was already ten times better than anything that ever happened in Leeds.

Lunchtime came around, and we went back to the common room to meet Mary. Scarlett went in to eat her lunch, and I raced off to the toilets. I came back into the room, smiling and ready to carry on where we left off, but I saw Scarlett sat on the black sofa next to Mary and three guys sat around her. The same guys who had glanced and whispered about her earlier in the morning.

They flirted with Scarlett and Mary, but with most of the attention directed at Scarlett. The guys joked with one another and showed off their new smartphones and clothes, all trying desperately to impress her and get one up on their friends.

I couldn't compete. I wore dingy clothes, my phone was worn and battered, and I didn't have their confidence or their muscles. I had been just lucky to get to talk to her first and come from the same place and do the same lessons.

I slumped, disappointed at the sight of the guys flirting with her, but I knew others were attracted to her. I couldn't keep her to myself all day. Tomorrow, we would have lessons together again, and maybe if my luck held out, she would talk to me again.

I walked off to the other side of the common room, picking my way through the tables of friends talking and joking together and sat at an empty desk to eat my lunch alone.

"Jon," I heard shouted across the room, and I turned around.

Scarlett waved me over. I headed back again around people eating their lunches, not sure what to expect on my arrival. I stood in front of her, just behind the guys circling her on the sofas. The guys turned around and glared at me for interrupting.

"Sorry boys, I promised to show Jon around today, maybe another time." Scarlett picked up her lunch and made her way out of the circle, forcing her admirers to move out of the way. I didn't hide the expression of smugness as the group of guys continued to glare at me with more intent.

Scarlett strode across the room and placed herself down at the empty table. I followed Scarlett back to the table, grinning as I went. Mary had stayed, enjoying all the attention to herself and flirted back.

"Are you sure?" I asked Scarlett as I sat down next to her.

"Hey. What do you mean?" she replied and looked surprised.

"You can have lunch with those guys if you want. I think I can find my way about now."

She smiled. "No thanks. I want to have lunch with you."

I must have looked startled, as though that was the strangest thing anyone had ever said.

"Is everything okay? I take it's all right to have lunch together still. I thought we were getting on well," she said, as she paused with the lid of her lunch box half-opened.

"We are getting along. I just didn't want to assume," I said, not wanting to give her the wrong impression and pleased this morning wasn't just a show, but the beginning of a genuine friendship.

#

We continued to hang around together during college time and started meeting up at weekends. Scarlett and Mary hadn't made many other friends since joining, and as all new to the area, it made sense to stick together. We would meet up to revise, as we shared many of the same classes anyway. We texted each other in the evenings and weekends, keeping the conversation from the day progressing.

I invited Scarlett and Mary to go to the cinema to see the latest sci-fi blockbuster. One night we connected to each other online playing "Crisis Red" and teamed up against a couple of kids from Scotland. We had become close friends in a relatively short space of time. Only a few weeks had passed, and I couldn't imagine life without her. However, things started to change.

One Friday afternoon, I hid in the art room, trying to do some homework when my phone beeped.

"Where are you?" Scarlett's message read.

I didn't answer. I had hidden from her on purpose. In those early weeks, I tried to put all thoughts of an intimate relationship with her out of my mind. We were friends and any clumsy attempt would ruin everything. Yet, my dreams wouldn't comply and undermined any efforts of friendship. The dreams weren't all explicit for eighteen years or over. Most were just Scarlett and me as a couple doing ordinary things, like watching the TV snuggled up together on the sofa. These dreams had the most profound effect. I would wake up full of spirits, bouncing out of bed and getting ready to meet her, and then remembered it wasn't real. The rest of the day, I would spend struggling to talk to her properly, as though we had been going out together and I had been dumped. I felt heartbroken and stupid knowing it had never been real and would never be real.

I continued on these happy dreams as daydreams, imagining what life would be like with Scarlett. Thoughts of our life together, like getting a flat, going out on the town, and then going to university together. I ran through every possibility in my mind and lived hundreds of different lives with her. I imagined every scenario I could possibly think of that she would suddenly want to be my girlfriend. Maybe I could win the lottery, be the lead singer in a band, inherit a fortune, or save her life. I decided it would need something dramatic and life-altering for her to see me in a new way.

My depression had lifted when we became friends. I had brightened up my outlook on life, and my clothes and attitude had likewise followed. However, the reality of our friendship began to hit home. I feared I would change into that sad guy following around a gorgeous girl, having to watch her date idiot after idiot while wishing she would one day notice me beyond just a friend. Everyone else would talk about me behind my back. I could imagine the snide comments.

"He doesn't stand a chance."

"She will only ever see him as a friend."

"It's so sweet. He is like a little puppy dog the way he follows her about."

I didn't want that to happen. My feelings for her had gotten out of control. I had become obsessed with her and would count the time between our meetings, inventing reasons to meet up.

I had enough, and I hid away from her between lessons, inventing reasons to disappear, or I would skip lessons to avoid the issue. That day I had hidden in the art room.

The phone beeped again.

"Jon, where are you?" the message read.

I tried again to keep studying, but daydreams of her kept overwhelming my concentration, and I stared into space instead. I fantasised I became a superhero by some sudden biological trigger, and I would save her life from vicious thugs. Just then, the door of the art room swung open. Scarlett came in, looked around and spotted me. The embarrassment jolted me out of my stupid fantasies, and I dipped my head into my books, trying to hide my flushed cheeks.

"So this is where you are hiding from me," she said, picking her way through the empty desks.

My heart pounded as she drew closer. I put my hand on my chest and felt it beating its exaggerated rhythm. "I'm not hiding. I was doing some homework."

"You could do that with me in the sixth form room."

"Sorry, I didn't want to bother you, and I have lots to do," I said, pretending to be deeply engrossed in my textbook, but sweat coated my skin, signalling my desperation for her.

"You wouldn't be bothering me. Why do you keep hiding?" she asked.

As she spoke, I fixated on her lips, watching them shape the words, squeezing in and pushing out, wishing I could lean forward and press my lips against hers. I wiped the sweat from my forehead. "Oh, just family issues. Sorry, I am not much company. I didn't want to bring you down."

"Are you sure? Don't lie to me," she said, raising one eyebrow and frowning a little.

"Honest, just a bit tense between Dad and I since moving to London," I said, and she seemed to believe it.

"Hmm. I am not sure. Anyway, let's go for a coffee in town on the way home. The house is empty tomorrow. Why don't you come around? I have already invited Mary. Maybe we could finally watch Star Wars together," she said, and waved me up and shut my textbooks.

"Okay, that would be great," I replied.

She wasn't going to leave me alone, so I did as she requested. Plus, the idea of going around her house excited me and had dampened the will to study. I packed up my books, happy she had sought me out, and that I would finally get to go around to her house.

CHAPTER FIVE

The next day, Saturday, I walked through the housing estate to Scarlett's to meet up with her and Mary. Scarlett's Mum had left for the weekend with her new boyfriend, so Scarlett had the house to herself. My phone vibrated in my pocket.

"Mary is ill and not coming. Just the two of us." Scarlett's message read.

I felt elated at the thought of having Scarlett to myself all day but also worried about the intensity of it. What if I couldn't cope without saying something stupid and giving away my true feelings for her? I would be alone with her all day in her house, and my imagination ran wild.

I texted Mary and wished her well, half hoping I could convince her to still come, so I could avoid the issue.

My phone rang, and Mary's name flashed across the screen.

"Hi Mary, you okay?" I answered.

"Yeah, I am fine actually. I am not ill at all. Just want to leave you two alone for the day."

"Hey, what do you mean?"

"Don't be dumb," she said, "you two have been dancing around it ever since you met. For goodness' sake, do us all a favour and get on with it. I can't stand the tension any longer."

"What do you mean?" I asked again, not believing what she was implying.

"She never stops talking about you, Jon. And you so obviously fancy her. You go all gooey-eyed every time you talk to her."

"I don't. We are just friends," I replied, embarrassed by the transparency of my feelings.

"You do fancy her, but Scarlett can't seem to see it and needs constant reassurance."

"Well, what do I do?"

"Just tell her the truth. One of you is going to have to break the silence."

"But what if she says no, or I mess it up?"

"She won't say no. You just need to take that gamble. Best of luck, Jon. Text me later if anything happens, bye," she said and hung up.

I walked in a daze, head spinning from the news, stumbling into a litterbin, and then bumping into an old lady walking her little dog. The dog yapped, and I apologised. I sat on a wall to regain my composure.

Scarlett fancying me! No way!

Mary must have made a mistake or maybe not. She seemed remarkably insistent and was rarely wrong. I smiled and held my head up high. I set off again and increased the pace, imagining what the rest of the day might hold. On the way, I revisited my favourite daydreams about being Scarlett's boyfriend. Maybe I didn't need to daydream anymore.

I stood outside the front door of Scarlett's house, brushed down my clothes, and tidied up my hair before ringing the bell. I wore the blue polo shirt she helped me choose yesterday after we went for a coffee, and I had put on my best jeans and carried a black fleece. I took a deep breath and tried to relax and look casual, but my nerves twitched, my eyebrows flickering.

"Just act normal," I repeated to myself.

The door opened. I took one look at Scarlett and wanted to drop to my knees to pledge my undying love to her straight away. I hoped Mary was right about Scarlett fancying me, else today would be the most torturous day of my life.

Scarlett was dressed to destroy. Her flame-red hair perfectly brushed into flowing locks over her shoulders, framing her face and light green eyes. She smiled, and her full lips lifted her cheeks and wrinkled her eyes in genuine pleasure to see me.

She wore a low-cut white lacy t-shirt, showing off her pushed up cleavage. The t-shirt came up short around her midriff and revealed her flat stomach and pierced belly button. After the flesh of her stomach, a snug pair of red hot pants sat on her hips, with the tops of her hip bones poking above the waistband. She had finished off with shocking red lips, fingernails, and toenails. Her legs were bare and shiny, with a thin silver chain rested on her left ankle. I stood in silence, stunned by her appearance and tried hard to hold my resolve.

"You're wearing the shirt we picked. It looks good," she said, running her hand gently through her flame-red hair.

"Thanks." I gulped. "You look lovely," I said, feeling I should recognise the effect she had on me.

"Do you think? Just some clothes I had lying about. Come in. I am glad you could still make it," she said.

"Of course, we can still have fun, just the two of us."

"This way," she said and walked upstairs to her bedroom.

I kicked off my shoes and followed her up the stairs. I walked behind, at head height to her red hot pants, and noticed a tattoo on the small of her back, a pair of extended silver and gold angel wings. As she moved up the stairs, her hips bounced up and down, giving the illusion of the wings moving. If Mary were wrong, it would be a long day.

Scarlett lived in a two-bedroom, beautifully decorated, semi-detached house on a new estate. Her home felt warm and shone clean and tidy. A pinewood fragrance filled the air rather than the musty smell of old socks we had in mine. I felt embarrassed by the state of my own house and would need to tidy it up if I ever invited her around.

In her bedroom, posters of sci-fi films and heavy metal bands covered her walls. The other students in the college would have guessed her room to be pink with posters of boy bands. Everything about Scarlett contradicted what everyone thought about her and the image she portrayed.

We listened to some classic heavy metal albums and sang along in her bedroom. Scarlett's vibrant red hair bounced about as she threw her head around to the music. I hoped Mary was right. Enclosed in her bedroom, the intensity between us grew. My heart pounded faster than ever before, heating me up, so I unbuttoned my polo shirt to let the air in. I tried my best to keep the conversation going, repeating things discussed only the day before, but uncomfortable silences kept breaking any momentum I developed to talk about our relationship. Scarlett spoke very little, so I tried hard to engage her in conversation. I couldn't decide if it was boredom or fear that kept her unusually quiet. My phone beeped to signal a text.

"Just tell her the truth," Mary's message said.

Scarlett's phone beeped next. I guessed Scarlett's message came from Mary, from the way she shielded her phone on receiving it and the look I got after she read it.

Scarlett got up and ran off to the toilet, from where I heard more beeps. She then reappeared at the bedroom door.

"You want a drink?" she asked.

"Tea, please."

She ran downstairs, and I could hear voices. I guessed Scarlett was making secret phone calls to Mary. It wasn't just me that was getting uncomfortable and acting strange. Maybe there was some truth in Mary's comments. I hoped it was Mary on the phone, encouraging Scarlett to tell the truth as well. Perhaps it explained her behaviour.

"Do you want to come downstairs and watch a film?" Scarlett shouted.

"Coming," I replied and walked down the stairs looking at the photos of her and her Mum on the wall. All the photos were recently taken, with nothing from her past before London.

I sat on a soft fabric beige sofa in front of the TV, and Scarlett entered carrying tea and snacks. We watched Star Wars together, sharing a bowl of tortilla chips between us. Occasionally, our hands touched as we reached in, and it sent a tingle through my arm. The film helped relieve the pressure of making conversation and avoided the tension between us. The film finished and neither of us said anything. I just stared at the credits, waiting for inspiration.

Scarlett moved the empty bowl and slid across the sofa.

"Jon, I'm glad Mary isn't here today, as I have something I want to talk to you about."

It sounded promising, and I sat up straight, anticipating what she would say next.

"Yeah, what's that?"

She took a deep breath.

"Why do you keep ignoring me and running off?" she asked.

It wasn't the question I expected. I sank into the sofa and answered the same way I had always answered.

"I told you before, just family issues," I said, feeling deflated.

"No, don't lie to me anymore. I know it's something to do with me."

"No, it's really not."

"Yes, it is. Just tell me the truth," she asked again, and reached out and held my hand.

I tried to pull away, but she gripped harder as my resistance increased.

"You have to face up to it. You can't be scared all the time," she said, staring into my eyes.

My gaze focused on her beautiful light green eyes. I felt scared and wanted to run, but she just held my hand tighter every time I tried to move away. It had been hard enough not saying something before. I had itched to tell her in the past but always seen sense at the last minute, not wanting to ruin our friendship.

I looked away, unable to take the pressure and stared at the floor. I wanted it to be true. I wanted to tell her everything, but she might laugh at the idea. She squeezed my hand gently, prompting and reminding me of her presence. I had said to myself when I moved to London, it would be a new me, not scared anymore, a fresh start. I had to tell her, even if it went badly. I had to be a new person else the O'Keefes would win.

"Yes, you're right. I can't do this anymore," I said, taking a deep breath, and I gripped her hand back but couldn't look her in the eyes.

"I hide because I find it hard to be around you," I said, not realising how it sounded.

"What's wrong with me?" she answered, pulling her hand back, but I held it tight.

"Nothing, that's the point. You are gorgeous and funny, and I enjoy spending all my time with you."

"So what's the problem?"

I would have to spell it out for her. I looked up, straight into her green eyes and faced the truth.

"I am attracted to you and want to be more than just friends."

I finally got it out and for a few seconds, I felt the pressure of my emotions disappear, but then I became worried. She squeezed my hand again and smiled.

"So why didn't you say before?"

"Just look at you. Let's face it, you're way out of my league. First, you're nearly two years older than I am. Second, there are much better-looking guys wanting to go out with you. And you're gorgeous, and funny, and could do much better than me," I rambled at her, repeating myself, but I kept my focus on her eyes.

Scarlett leant forward, brushing away my hair draped over the side of my face.

"There is a handsome man under all that hair and gloom," she said. "You are a real friend, not like the others in the class. They only pretend. They are only after one thing."

"I am hardly popular or fashionable like you," I said, embarrassed by her affection, and my face glowed from her gentle touch across my cheek.

"I wish I had the guts to dress how I honestly felt, but I am too scared of what others would think," she said.

She then looked at me for a long time, not saying a word, weighing up the situation.

"Let me show you something."

Scarlett pulled out a photo album from the shelves and pointed at some pictures of her at school in Leeds. I didn't recognise her. Where she pointed on the picture stood a girl with brown hair, thick glasses, and fat pushing out against her school uniform. She looked like a geek.

"Yes, that's me."

I did the double-take from photo to her and back. Scarlett smiled, apparently used to this reaction.

"I lost my appetite during my parents' divorce. Things were difficult. Mum wanted out of Leeds and found a job in London, so we moved. She reinvented herself, became a new person," she said.

I looked at the photo and then at Scarlett again, still taking it in, finding it hard to believe. "I did the same. I decided to live up to my name of Scarlett, dyed my hair, changed my image, stayed on a diet to keep the weight off, and got contact lenses."

Scarlett took the photo album, shoved it back on the shelves, out of her sight like a memory she wished to forget. She then rejoined me on the sofa and held my hand.

"What did I look like, Jon?" she asked.

"An ordinary girl."

She raised her eyebrows and looked at me sternly.

"Say what you really thought."

"A geek," I responded and tried to smile the insult away.

"Yes, I was. I still am," she answered back, "this is just an image," she said, waving at her clothes and hair. "I have never had a proper boyfriend, and I am guessing you never had a girlfriend either."

"Not really," I answered.

"This isn't easy for me, either. I am as scared as you. I thought you'd gone off me by hiding away."

"No, I haven't. It just felt easier to avoid it. I hoped the time apart would make it easier but it didn't. I just missed you more."

"Can't run scared all your life," she said and shuffled towards me on the sofa. "I want us to be more than friends as well," she said, tilting her head to one side. Her flame-red hair cascaded to reveal her vulnerable neck while her light green eyes kept their gaze on mine.

It's actually happening, I said to myself over and over. I was no expert in signals from girls, but even I had seen enough films to know what to do next. I shuffled along the sofa, removing the final space between us, and put my arm around her. We looked into each other's eyes for a few moments. Her pupils dilated into dark pools, and her red lips summoned me.

We leant into each other's embrace and edged forwards with our heads tilting around. Our lips finally connected. We started kissing. I put my arms around her waist and pulled her in closer. She moved with the flow, wrapping her arms around me and kissing me back. I shook in ecstasy. My heart felt as if it would break my bones as it hammered on the walls of my ribcage. All of my daydreams had come true. I couldn't believe it was actually happening.

When we finally stopped kissing, we just stared into one another's eyes for a while. Not sure what to do next. I decided I should come clean on my past life, just as she had done. I wanted to be a new person, and I had to face the truth. I needed someone to share it with.

"There is something I should tell you about Leeds. The real reason my Dad and I left."

"So there is something else going on?"

"The incident you talked about. The gang kidnapping a kid. That was my best friend they took. I was in the car when it ran into the gang."

"Oh my. You poor thing."

"That isn't the worse of it. They bullied my friend afterwards as revenge. Actually, they always bullied us, but now he got all their attention and it got worse."

"You must have suffered. So you left because of the bullying?"

"Yes and no. There is more. When they took him from the gates at the school, I should have stopped them, but I was scared. They hit me and scared me away. I called Giles' Mum and got the caretaker to help search for him."

"How would you have stopped them? I heard they did this in broad daylight. Parents and teachers walked away. It was a big scandal in the papers about the lack of adult intervention. A failure of big society."

"I am not sure. I should have just refused to leave."

"I don't think it would have made any difference. I reckon they would have just beaten you and then left anyway. No adult was going to stop them, so I doubt if you could."

"Regardless, he was my best friend. I should have tried harder. I should have let myself get beaten up, even if it was for nothing. I should have proved my loyalty."

"It would have been pointless. I think you did the right thing by getting help."

Having someone on my side made a big difference. I smiled for a moment. "But I haven't finished. When they bullied him at school afterwards, I had abandoned him. My Dad told me it had been agreed with his father to keep apart. He said it was something about the court case of the kidnapping and car accident. I left him to the gang. It was this bullying that drove him to suicide."

"Oh. You feel it was your fault he tried to kill himself."

"Yes. I should have been a better friend."

"They would have targeted you as well. But regardless of your actions, whether they were right or wrong, it is only them to blame for hurting him. I am not sure why you had to keep apart."

"I think my Dad made it up. I think he told Giles' family that he didn't want me involved. My Dad took away my phone and internet connection so I couldn't explain when out of school. I couldn't get close enough during school hours to tell him. The O'Keefe gang had him under surveillance the whole time."

"After the suicide, you left for London?"

"Our house was attacked the same night Giles tried to kill himself. We got a brick through the window and graffiti scrolled across the door. It was obvious I was their next target. I think they knew I was giving evidence against them at the court case. We moved house, and I homeschooled until the exams, and then we left for London. My Dad had been offered a new job."

"That is terrible. I was bullied as well. You saw the photo. I was the fat geek girl, an easy target. Everyone joined in, as it meant they weren't targeted. So I know what it was like. Although I realise it wasn't as bad," she said and hugged me.

I hugged her back and we just held each other. She tried to let go but I held tight, as reliving the incident brought tears to my eyes, and I didn't want her to see me crying. After a few more moments, I let go and wiped my eyes, and I had left a damp spot of tears on her vest top. She looked into my eyes and smiled, and then pulled a tissue out of her pocket and handed it to me.

"Do you want a cup of tea?" she said.

"Yes, please."

She went into the kitchen, giving me a chance to get myself together.

The rest of the day went well. Scarlett texted Mary to tell her the news, and then we just enjoyed each other's company without the tension. Just like an average couple doing normal things together. We watched the next Star Wars film and snuggled up on the sofa together, just as I had dreamt. We kissed more, shared our feelings about how we felt and how it all started, and we laughed about our terrible attempts at coming out with the truth.

The next morning, I woke up and remembered it was real, not my subconscious trying to destroy me, but life finally rewarding me. I had never been happier. I bounced out of bed, racing to get dressed to get back over to Scarlett's house for my first full day as her boyfriend.

CHAPTER SIX

I'd been dating Scarlett for a couple of weeks in secret, only Mary knew. But we decided not to hide it anymore while at college. As Scarlett and I walked across to the front gates, the wind picked up the leaves and continually shuffled them into different piles across the courtyard. Mary wandered behind us, listening to her iPod and giving us a little space, happy she didn't have to play piggy in the middle anymore.

Through the gates, a gang hung about waiting for friends and getting up to no good. Scarlett and Mary had warned me about this gang on the first day I arrived; they were called the "Rude Crew." I had no issues with them, and I had kept well out of their way, taking the long routes around to stay out of their sight. That day, Mary and Scarlett wanted to go shopping nearby, and this was the direct route. Probably because of my newly found confidence, I strode through the front gates hand-in-hand with Scarlett.

The gang contained six ex-students who hung around harassing the kids from the school while selling drugs, drinks and stolen goods. Barry McGowan, the gang leader, sat on his mountain bike in the middle of the action, and the others vied for his attention. By the look of his hardened craggy face, his twenty years of life had been full of fighting. His black puffer jacket covered his thick body frame, which contrasted to his blond shaven head and high thick forehead. Out the back of his coat, the ever-present gang hoodie hung. Barry looked like a thug.

In contrast to Barry, Tony was the youngest member of the gang, and his clothes hung off his tall, lean frame. The others in the gang ranged in ages between Tony and Barry. They all wore black or blue jeans, jackets, trainers or boots, and hoodies either over their heads or hanging down. The others in the gang were John, George, Mike, and Andy.

Mike rode on his skateboard and Andy on his bike, shouting and crashing into people as they hopelessly tried to perform tricks. Andy's face carried a few cuts and bruises. The sides of his hair were shaven and short blond spikes formed a strip down the middle. Mike had perfectly styled hair and a clean-shaven face. He obviously spent a lot of time grooming his looks.

To the side, John and George huddled together with a student making a drug transaction. John, the second in command, was thickset and muscular with light brown hair in a long ponytail. George was small and wiry, head and eyes flitting about like a meerkat. Their hands quickly swapped money and small wraps of paper while they looked around furtively for teachers or police. In the centre of it all, Barry sat on his bike, lusting at the girls walking past and keeping an eye on the general goings on.

The noise of the gang drowned out the sounds of the other students, and as we walked past, I couldn't help but look over. At that moment, Barry caught my eye and nudged Tony. They whispered and then looked over at me again. I pulled my head around quickly and continued to walk off. I didn't want to get involved. I had enough of gangs in Leeds. I just wanted a quiet life. I didn't care that they sold drugs or stole stuff from other students. It wasn't my concern. I'd learnt my lessons in Leeds.

I walked on, picking up the pace, pulling Scarlett and Mary with me. If I left and didn't look back, it would show I wasn't interested; it would show them I wasn't worth the bother. I reached the corner and turned around to look back. Tony and John were stalking me. Too late.

I kept striding on when Scarlett hauled me back.

"Why you in such a rush?" she asked.

"I have attracted the attention of that gang. Some of them are following me," I replied, and glanced back at them again. My new confidence started melting away and the same anxieties I felt when at school in Leeds crept back.

She peered around, glimpsed them catching up with us, turned back and grabbed my arm.

"Just keep walking," she said and pressed forward.

We moved through the rest of the kids walking home, but they still followed. We tried to escape by running down a deserted alley. Our legs cut through the cold autumn air, whipping up the leaves and rubbish, which stuck to our feet as we ran. They saw us and chased, their feet slapping the ground behind us.

I let the girls run ahead, as we weren't far from a shopping area and relative safety in public view. As they ran, Scarlett's bag slipped off her shoulder and wrapped around my legs. My feet tangled up in the shoulder strap, and I stumbled and tripped. I flew forwards, stretching my hands out before me and shielding the blow from my face. My hands took the blow and burnt against the rough pavement, and I rolled forward onto my back, trying to take the momentum out of the fall. I shook my legs loose of the strap, but Tony and John had already made up the ground and now stood either side of me.

"In a rush, are we?" Tony asked.

"It's not nice running off. We just wanted to meet you," John added.

I stood up, picked up Scarlett's pink bag and went to walk past them, but

Tony blocked my path with his arm.

"Hey, where are you going with your pretty little bag?" he asked.

"With my friends," I replied, and looked straight past him to the end of the alley, knowing I wasn't far away from safety.

"You're not from around here, are you? You're new. Where are you from?"

"Leeds," I responded.

I tried to play it cool, just give them easy answers, and maybe I could get away with a warning. Maybe I could walk away from here in a few seconds with just my ears ringing with abuse and threats. I would be happy with that, not a pleasant way to finish the day but better than others.

"Hey John, we've got a northerner here. What are you doing here? I don't remember you asking us," Tony said.

"What?"

"Listen to him. What do you sound like?" he said and laughed, and John sighed with disapproval.

"Just leave me alone," I said, and I tried to walk past Tony again, hoping it would prove my lack of interest.

"No. I won't leave you alone. What are you doing with that girl?"

He grabbed hold of my coat collars and pushed me back into John, who placed his hands on my shoulders and held me firm.

"She's my girlfriend," I responded, not expecting this question.

"No way," he laughed, "you don't get to go out with one of our girls."

"She's not from around here either. She's from Leeds, like me," I said.

Tony punched me in the stomach. "Not anymore she isn't. She is one of ours."

I doubled up in pain and put a hand to the floor to regain my balance. I should have let that be it, but my anger grew. I didn't want to give her up. I wanted to be a proper man, not scared anymore. Being with Scarlett was the best thing that had ever happened to me, and I would not let it be ruined by anyone. I wouldn't be bullied again.

I stood up and pushed my hands up through Tony's arms, forcing him to release me, and then stamped backwards onto John's foot. He shouted and let go of my shoulders. I slipped the bag off my shoulder and swung it into Tony's stomach, knocking the breath out of him, and then I ran off down the alley.

They chased after me, but I could tell I had gained enough ground. They would never catch me before the safety beyond the alleyway, passed a few houses, and around the corner into the shopping area. I turned the corner at the end, and I slammed straight into someone on a bike.

We tumbled over and the bike crashed around over both our heads. I scrambled onwards, with my hands and feet pulling myself back upright, and went to run off, not caring about who I'd hit. But a hand grabbed my shoulder and threw me back across the pedals of the bike. The pedals ripped through my jacket and cut into my back as I rolled off onto the pavement. I looked up and saw the gang leader, Barry McGowan. His face scowled and grazed, and his fists clenched. Tony and John quickly gained ground down the alley.

"Where you going, boy?" Barry yelled.

I got to my feet and went to run off again when something heavy pounded onto my back. I collapsed with my face flat against the concrete.

"What's going on?" Barry asked Tony as John got to his feet from knocking me to the floor.

"The new kid took us by surprise," he said while catching his breath.

Barry looked down and frowned.

"Going to teach you a lesson new boy."

Barry kicked my stomach, and I wrapped my arms around it and shouted in pain. The others followed suit, and I couldn't defend myself from the barrage of flying feet. The kicks rained in, and I tried moving away, but they wouldn't let me go and started spitting in my face.

"Loser," Tony shouted.

Barry got out his phone and started recording. "Another hit for YouTube, boys." He laughed aloud, and they laughed with him as they posed for the camera and then kicked me.

"We are going to make you famous, new boy," Tony shouted.

The kicking seemed to last forever, and I hoped that someone would stop them, a teacher, police, other students or Scarlett and Mary. No one came. The houses nearby must have had people in, but they did nothing either.

They stopped, and Barry leant in with his phone to get a closeup of my battered face.

"Welcome to London, new boy," he said, "now give me your money and phone."

Tony pushed me onto my back and routed through my pockets, finding my mobile and wallet.

"You go to the police loser, and I will wait for you every day, and your girlfriend," Barry said as he stopped filming, and then finished his sentence by punching my nose.

My head rocked back and slammed into the pavement behind. My nose burst open, and the blood ran down my face, mixing in with the streaming tears of pain and humiliation, and their dribbles of spit.

Through the haze of blood and tears, I saw them saunter back down the alleyway. Money passed between them. Barry replayed the video of my attack, and they laughed at it.

CHAPTER SEVEN

Once the gang disappeared, Scarlett and Mary reappeared. Scarlett ran over and cradled my head in her lap, while trying to wipe away the blood from my face with the sleeve of her shirt. Tears rolled down her face and dripped onto mine. Her beautiful red hair billowed in the wind and wrapped around her tear-stained face. Mary assumed the role of nurse. She asked me where it hurt and checked to see if any bones were broken. People from the houses appeared as well, but Scarlett screamed, "Oh, now you come out. Just get lost. We can manage on our own."

Scarlett held me as tight as possible, putting pressure on my bruises.

"It will be okay. I will look after you," she said as we both kept crying. I wanted to scream in pain from the pressure, but the words meant so much to me. I just let it be and held her close, not wanting to let go.

They helped me to my feet, put their arms around me, and then walked me back to Scarlett's house. I sat on the beige fabric sofa in Scarlett's front room and clutched an ice bag to my bruised face. Mary cleaned up my wounds and gave me some painkillers. Scarlett did her best to make me feel better by holding my hand and kissing me gently on the cheeks every couple of minutes. It felt nice but it didn't work. Instead, I shook all over from the pain and adrenaline. I wanted Barry and his gang to suffer. I wanted to hear their bones break so I could laugh at them. I wanted revenge. I wanted them dead.

I stayed at Scarlett's house as long as possible, not wanting to go home to an empty house, not wanting to burden my Dad with the latest instalment of my troubled life. Scarlett put a film on and sat at the end of the sofa. I slumped down, cuddled into her and rested my head on her chest with her arm wrapped around my shoulder. Mary had busied herself texting and decided to leave us to it and to head home before it got too late.

A few minutes later, the front door opened, and I guessed it was Jill, Scarlett's Mum, coming home from work. We had met a couple of days after I started dating Scarlett, and she seemed nice, friendly and welcoming whenever I came around. I had stopped over for dinner and watched TV with them when Dad worked late. She walked in dressed in her smart office clothes to say hello and immediately noticed the bruises on my face.

"What happened?" she asked.

"A gang attacked him just outside the school," Scarlett added, without giving me a chance to lie.

"Why?"

"We don't know. I think because he is new. They took his money and phone."

"Have you called the police yet?"

"Not calling the police. I don't want any more trouble," I answered, fixing my eyes on the TV.

"You can't let them get away with it. Do you know who did it?" she asked.

"Yes I do, but they will come back after me if I grass on them. I don't want to get either of us into more trouble."

"You should tell the police. This is how these gangs get away with it. It needs people to stand up to them," she said.

After the events in Leeds, I didn't want to go back down that route again. I just wanted to forget about it and hoped it would be a one-off event. I still had to face the O'Keefes in the courtroom. I could do without going through the same distress again in my new home. I doubted I would get another offer of protection, so I had to make the best of my new life in London. At least in London, I had Scarlett.

Jill looked at the bruises some more and continued to advise me to go to the police, but I could still hear Barry's warnings in my ears about what would happen if I grassed on them. I knew from previous experience what could happen if I did. Memories of events in Leeds flashed back in my mind, and I remembered the hell Giles and his family went through, and the constant fear I suffered as well. I didn't want to reach the point where I would slit my wrists in a warm bath, just as Giles did to escape his torment.

"I better get home," I answered, not wanting to argue about it anymore.

Jill sighed, knowing it was a lost cause.

"Let me run you home at least," she said.

"Thank you, that would be great," I answered, got up and checked my pockets for my house keys.

I couldn't find them. I frantically padded every pocket and turned out their contents onto the table, but they were gone.

"My keys have gone. I must have lost them, or they were taken," I said.

"What about your Dad?" Jill asked.

"He will have some. Can you drop me off at his workplace instead?"

"Of course."

The three of us got into Jill's black Mini Cooper. Scarlett and I sat in the back, holding hands while I gave directions.

I would have to face my Dad. We thought our problems had been left behind in Leeds, but it would seem I was destined to be a victim all my life. My Dad would have to suffer my fate.

CHAPTER EIGHT

We arrived at the research facility, a large grey concrete structure with a barrier across the only entrance, and armed guards in a cabin at the side of the barrier. A high barbed wire electric fence ringed the centre. This wasn't the sort of place you just walked into uninvited.

I kissed Scarlett goodbye and clambered out of the car, being careful not to hit my bruises. The guards watched me suspiciously, taking in the bruises and blood on my clothes and face as I hobbled over. They opened the cabin door.

"Hi, can you call my father, Dr Clarence Watson?"

"Of course. Who should I say is asking?"

"His son, Jon."

One guard typed into a computer and then dialled on a white phone.

"Dr Watson? Your son is at the front gate."

The guard ushered me into the cabin and handed over the phone.

"Hi, Dad."

"Jon, what is going on?"

"I am sorry to disturb you, but on the way home, I got attacked. They stole my money and phone, and I think my house keys."

He grunted and sighed. "Hand over the phone to the guards."

I handed it back

"Yes, sir," the guard said and hung up.

"He will be up in a few minutes. It's a little bit of a trek from his research area."

I thanked the guard and returned to the car and waited in the back seat with Scarlett.

After ten minutes, he exited the main reception door and walked across the empty car park. He wore his white lab coat with ID badge attached, black trousers, black shoes, and his small rounded spectacles. He bent down to the open front passenger window and looked inside at me, and then turned to Jill. "Thank you for taking care of him. I am sorry to have troubled you. I will look after him now."

"It's no problem. He can stop at ours for the night if you are busy."

"No, we couldn't trouble you anymore. I will look after him. Thank you for the offer. Jon, let's go."

I turned to Scarlett, who kissed me. "Take care. Call me."

I gave her a hug and got out of the car. I waved goodbye to them, and Scarlett blew me a kiss as a single tear rolled down her face. The car reversed around and drove off down the road.

We walked across the empty car park, and Dad ushered me inside the building out of the cold. We walked through the white marbled floor lobby, around an enclosed receptionist desk and down the endless empty white corridors. Empty offices and other corridors shot off the sides of the main corridor. Most people had already gone home, it being late at night.

The corridors got shorter and the offices smaller as we walked through.

"So, what happened?" Dad asked after a long silence.

"I was leaving with Scarlett, and the gang followed us. We tried to run for it, but I tripped over."

"So then they grabbed you?"

"Yes and they started harassing me, but I got away from them again until I ran into the gang leader."

"So you fought them?"

"Well, yeah, I suppose I did. I fought my way out from the first two but ran into the gang leader. By the time I recovered, they had me surrounded. They were annoyed I had almost got away the first time. They hit me to the floor and kicked me all over and then stole my phone, wallet and keys."

"Bloody gangs. You did well defending yourself. Hopefully, this will be a one-off."

He swiped his card again and placed his eye against a reader on the side panel. The elevator door opened and we entered. He pressed "B," for basement I guessed, and we descended into the depths of the building.

"I will sort out some arrangements to get you home," he said, "I have to work all night."

"I know, Dad."

The lift stopped, and we walked along a single corridor passed a couple of rooms, and then into his lab. The smell of fresh paint lingered in the air and a single bare bulb illuminated the room. As we entered, I noticed two needles filled with a red substance sat on the side. Dad shoved them in a drawer in the hope I hadn't noticed, which I wouldn't have but for him hiding them away.

"Sit here and don't touch anything. I am going to make some phone calls."

He sat me down in a chair in front of his computer by the side of a large tinted mirror. He looked at the repair work on my face and then walked into the office next door to make his calls, as he needed a fixed phone line this deep underground.

In the mirror, my reflection revealed the beating I had taken. My black eye had swollen and my nose bruised and bloodied, but most of the pain came from the rest of my body. My legs and back hurt like hell, as they had absorbed most of the kicks. I shuffled in the chair and tried to find a way of sitting that didn't hurt. I brushed at the dirt, blood, snot, tears, and spit that stained my clothes. Then I brushed my hair and straightened my clothes as I viewed my reflection, trying to get some dignity back. But again, I found myself staring into my own eyes, wondering how I had gotten into this mess and what the future held.

Next to the mirror was a control panel with various black buttons ran down the side. The rest of the room contained clinical white cupboards perched along the walls and black work surfaces, with drawers and cupboards underneath where the needles had been placed. Equipment sat on top of the work surfaces: microscopes, spinning things, folders, books, and cupboards full of scientific kit.

I looked back into the mirror, and my reflection disgusted me. I was a loser. Anger burned at my lack of strength. I thought about Giles and the fact we had saved him initially from what I had just been through. He never thanked me for getting his Mum and protecting him. He just blamed me for not being beaten up with him and for looking the other way and walking on. After moving all this way to avoid troubles at home, I had still ended up bruised, battered, hurt, and even more scared than before.

Also, I feared I lost Scarlett's respect along with my phone, money, and dignity. I had no reason to believe Scarlett would leave me. She had been upset and cared for me, but I wasn't thinking straight. She was too good for me, and I had always known this to be true. Eventually, someone older, braver and cooler would take an interest, and it would be the end. That evening, others had noticed her and were jealous enough to attack me to push me away.

My anger boiled inside. Why did all these dreadful things happen to me? What had I done to the world, so that everything kept being snatched away? From the very day I had been born, Mum died, and Dad resented me for the death of his wife and curtailing his work. Bullied at school from the very first day, the car accident with Giles' Mum and the O'Keefes harassing me. Then being mugged in London, just when I had finally started a new life for myself. I jumped off the chair and kicked it to the floor, and then punched a cupboard. Ouch. I cradled my hand as my bruised knuckles throbbed with pain.

"Blood and rage, how sweet," a soft feminine voice smoothly interrupted my self-loathing.

The voice sounded strange, the accent weird. It started off eastern

European and finished in French.

"Hello!" I answered back, looking around the room and down the corridor. I couldn't hear anyone else except my Dad talking in the office next door.

"Hello," I said again, nervously re-entering the room.

"Through the mirror," the voice replied.

I hadn't imagined it. The voice contained a strange mixture of harsh eastern tones, finishing in a sexy French voice. It then dawned on me that the voice sounded just in my head.

"Hello", I thought instead of speaking, and the image of the panel adjacent to the mirror appeared in my mind. Curious, I walked straight over and pressed the button it showed.

The tinted mirror cleared to glass, showing a small white painted room on the other side. Embedded into the ceiling, a series of strip lights illuminated the room in a flood of white light. A single bed with tatty unmade sheets was tucked into the far right corner.

A young woman in her late twenties walked back and forth across the room, dropping her eyes to the floor and passing either side of a bare wooden chair positioned in front of the mirror. As she walked, her boot heels tapped across the exposed wooden floorboards, and her long tousled raven hair bounced up and down on the shoulder straps of her figure-hugging white vest top. The light reflected off her tight, black, shiny combat trousers as she paced up and down like a captive animal wearing a groove in the floor. Her body, hugged by the tight-fitting clothes, held the perfect balance of curves across her tall, athletic frame. I stood frozen to the spot as I looked at my fantasy woman, and an instant blaze of desire swept through me.

"Hi," I said and waved pathetically to her, unsure what else to do.

She stopped and looked up at me. She looked sad; her face ashen and drooped, and her shoulders slumped forward. As our eyes met, her body straightened and pushed upright and firm, and her face came alive. Her features appeared flawless and well defined, creating perfect symmetry. Her bright sky blue eyes sparkled, and a small smile lifted her face, and her gaze penetrated straight through the glass and burned into my eyes and into my soul. I became transfixed, and I stared back at her without embarrassment. The surrounding noises faded away, and my vision of everything else blackened. My sight could only cope with the gorgeous vision of her as her presence dominated everything else, pushing it to the edges of my senses.

Her raven hair flowed backwards as if it had a life of its own. Her lips darken to a deep bloodied red, and her cheeks became flushed with colour. She emitted a brooding intensity that poured out as a mist, swirling around in the air and filling up the space between us. The mist built up against the glass, pushing against it, trying to find a way through.

The glass bulged against the mist seeping through the invisible spaces in the atoms; it cascading through like a waterfall and forming a pool lapping around my feet. It built up layer by layer, getting higher and higher, encircling and enveloping me. The hairs on my body rose as the hot mist formed ghostly tentacles, which grasped at my torso, arms and legs. Small shivers sparked up my back and into the pleasure sensors in my mind. The mist twisted into my nose, and its musky smell triggered a chemical reaction that engulfed my senses. I abandoned myself control, and desire swept through me. I burned up with pleasure and a desire to embrace her, no matter the consequences.

"Revenge, revenge," she whispered into my mind over and over again.

I watched transfixed, my mind utterly lost in a deep trance, absorbing every wave of pleasure. I ached to hold her tight and delight in her perfect body. Her hand stretched out, and she beckoned me towards her. The misty tentacles of her desire pulled me towards the glass and towards her. My hands braced against the glass, and my hot breath fogged up the window while I continued to absorb the vision in the other room.

"Revenge, revenge, my darling."

She glided towards the glass and lowered both straps on her vest top, revealing her bare shoulders. Another image flashed into my head of the two needles I had seen earlier. I shook, but my eyes kept transfixed on the goddess before me, as she pulled down the rest of her top to her waist. Her perfect body coated in a warm, inviting layer of moisture.

Strong ultraviolet light flooded the room from the ceiling. Her flesh burnt and smoke rose from the charred wounds. She screamed and dived across the room, trying to hide under the blanket on the bed. My thoughts became my own again, as I had been released from her possession. I rocked backwards and shook my head to break the rest of the spell. The lights went back to normal again, and my Dad released a button from the control panel. The mist had disappeared from the lab and the other room.

I looked back into the room, just in time to see the woman spring out from under the blanket and fling herself against the glass. It shuddered but withheld the battering. I bolted backwards and fell into the chair behind me as she snarled and screamed into the glass. Her face contorted and muscles jutted out as they spasmed and flexed while increasing in proportion. Her bright sky blue eyes flooded blood red, with cat-like black slits in the middle. Her hair wildly jutted out as it stood on its ends, and skin drained from flushed red cheeks and seduction red lips, to an aggressive, sick grey.

She snarled again, opened her mouth, and I saw the clinching point, a set of fangs dripping with saliva. My own colour drained away, and my heartbeat pounded in my ears. I stared glued to the glass as her hot snarling breath misted it up, and time faltered as I feared the glass would capitulate to her rage.

She screamed and bashed the glass with her fists and claws until the rage slowed. She took a couple of steps back. Her fangs retracted and blood-red eyes flashed back to her sky bright eyes but tears welled within. Her shoulders slumped and face drained. She had reverted to the sad and lonely woman I saw when I first looked through the glass. She turned, pulled up her vest top and walked back to the bed where she laid down. As she faced away from us, her burns healed in an instant to smooth, pale, unblemished skin.

"What the hell was that?" I asked, pointing at her.

My Dad pressed another button, and the glass reverted to a mirror.

"I said don't touch anything," he shouted back at me.

"It looks like a vampire."

"Never mind what it is. It was a mistake to bring you down here," he replied.

Two security guards dressed in grey combat overalls and black boots burst into the room with guns pointed at us.

My Dad put his hands in the air. "It's okay, no problems. She has been subdued."

He ushered them out the door back into the corridor. At that moment, the image of the two needles flashed across my mind again. She was trying to tell me something, just like she did with the button on the control panel. I didn't have time to think it through, and I realised I stood with my back to the drawer my Dad had placed them in earlier. I stayed facing the guards and reached behind me with one hand and eased open the drawer. I reached in, grabbed both needles and secreted them up the sleeve of my coat.

Dad turned around.

"Let's get you home before you cause any more damage," he said.

"Is it a vampire?" I asked again.

"You didn't see anything. Do you understand?" he shouted, grabbing my shoulders and shoving me back into the drawers.

"Okay, okay," I replied, not wanting any more bruises.

We made most of the journey back to the gate in silence. Neither of us looked at one another, both of us unsure of what to say. I guess out of remorse for shouting at me or desire to tell someone, my Dad started speaking.

"Vampire, I guess is the right word," he said out of the blue.

I looked up at him, waiting to hear more.

"We are studying her to develop genetic formulas that could benefit humankind."

"Or weapons," I responded.

He looked down his glasses at me. "Maybe."

"One of the formulas will give the taker the power of the vampire for just one night."

I placed my hand around the needles now in my coat pocket. It had to be these needles. Why else would she have shown them to me? But why me?

"Blood and anger," she had said at the beginning.

She sensed my anger, smelt my blood and wanted me to have revenge. Yes, revenge.

"Revenge, revenge, my darling," her voice sounded in my head again, although it grew fainter as we ascended.

I imagined her again, face ashen, drooped, and sad. I felt sympathy for her. I remembered the meeting of our eyes and her raven hair blowing in the wind. Her red lips seducing, body glistening, and the mist enticing me forward, and my desire drowning me. Next, the UV lights triggered her change to protruding fangs, fiery-red eyes and contorting muscles, as she smashed against the mirror and invoked my fear. Also, the sadness I encountered when released from her possession. In the end, her face ashen and walking back to the bed, sad and lonely again. I felt a connection, a shared sense of loneliness.

"What's her name?" I asked.

Dad looked at me puzzled and frowned at this question.

"What's her name?" I asked again.

"I don't know," he replied, perplexed. "She is just Subject X," he added as if this were an obvious, proper answer.

The rest of the journey back up to the entrance of the building carried on in silence, and we waited quietly outside until my lift arrived. My Dad had arranged a taxi to take me home and gave me his set of keys to get inside. As the taxi pulled up, he whispered in my ear.

"Remember. You saw nothing. My job and our safety rely on it. You must not tell anyone."

I nodded in reply but gripped the needles as I did. I didn't intend to tell anyone, but I did intend to show them.

CHAPTER NINE

I slept fitfully all night with dreams of the attack by the gang, the kicks in the back, and their snarling angry faces, spitting and shouting at me. Next, dreams of Subject X repeatedly whispering the word revenge, her raven hair blowing from an unknown breeze, her sky bright eyes dazzling me, and her warm glistening body seducing me. The UV lights switched on and she turned into a vampire with burning red eyes and snarling fangs. She smashed through the mirror and bit into my neck. I woke up dripping in sweat; it stinging my bruises, not sure what was real and what was a dream.

The attack was real, as the bruises all over my body acted as a painful reminder. The events in the basement must have been a dream, but under my bed, in my suitcase, a red needle was waiting and willing me to use it. The other needle I had hidden away under the floorboards for extra safekeeping in case something went wrong.

I stayed off college to recover, and I worried they would come after me again, or Scarlett, so I decided not to tell anyone who had done it. My mind floated back and forth between Subject X's image, sad to beautiful to angry and then sad again. The feelings of sympathy and desire I felt overwhelmed by when I fantasised about her. To feelings of anger and rage aimed at Barry and his gang.

The sick days ran straight into the weekend, and as time went on, the dreams of Subject X drifted away like a beautiful nightmare, and I thought of Scarlett again. Scarlett finally came around to see me on Saturday afternoon, two days after the attack. I had been emailing her and calling her the last two days but with no reply. Her lack of response proved she was embarrassed and had lost respect for me. She probably wanted a proper boyfriend that could look after her.

When she arrived, my emotions flipped back and forth between happy and angry. My Dad showed her in and she came up to my room, which I had hardly left over the last two days. I hadn't bothered to decorate my room when we came to London. Instead, I had just filled the room up with posters and pictures. The posters showed bands, films, and scantily clad women, which I had taken off the walls when I started dating Scarlett. The room had until recently been tidy, as I had tried my best to keep it clean for when Scarlett came around, but over the last few days, I had returned to my old ways and the room had descended into a mess. I paused my

Xbox and turned my music off as she climbed the stairs.

She tapped lightly on the door and gave an embarrassed smile as she walked in.

"Hi, how you doing?" she asked, looking sheepish.

I couldn't be bothered with the niceties, but even though I felt angry with her, I still couldn't help noticing how beautiful she looked. Her flame red hair tied back, and her green eyes dilated as they adjusted to the darkly lit room. She wore her tight blue jeans and a white t-shirt saying "RED" across her chest in red brick texture letters.

"Where have you been?" I snapped.

"I thought it just best to leave you alone for a couple of days. My Mum didn't want me going out after what happened," she replied.

I looked away as I realised it was probably true.

"Stopped you using your phone and computer as well?" I asked.

She stared down at the floor, with no excuse forthcoming.

"Sorry, I didn't know what to say. It felt a bit weird after what happened," she said.

My fears confirmed. She was embarrassed and didn't want to associate herself with me anymore.

"Oh great, not only did you get me into this, but now you don't want to talk to me either," I said, spitting out the words.

"What? I didn't do this."

"It's your fault. They told me you're one of their girls. It's the way you dress. What did you expect?"

"What the hell. You seem pretty happy about it normally, getting the girl the other boys wanted. I have seen you strutting around. Anyway, I can dress how the hell I want."

"You should have some self-respect, and you dropped that damn bag as well, which tripped me up."

"Oh, it's all my fault, is it?" she retorted, eyes narrowing and glaring, with her hands on her hips. "Get some guts. Stuff just happens so deal with it," she shouted.

"You left me there alone. Let me get beaten up. They may have left me alone if you were there."

"Just like you did with Giles," she snapped back with venom.

"Get lost," I screamed in disbelief that she had thrown that in my face. I told her that in confidence, my deepest darkest secret.

"With pleasure," she said, crashing out of my room and slamming the door, shaking the pictures on the wall and leaving a ringing in my ears. She thumped down the stairs, shoved her boots and coat on, and then slammed the front door.

"Bye, Scarlett," Dad shouted out.

I sulked for the rest of the day, not sure what to do. The anger returned stronger than before, and images of Subject X flooded back to the forefront of my mind. I pictured her through the glass: sad, beautiful and terrifying, all in the space of a couple of moments.

I'd not slept much over the last two nights, too many strange dreams of vampires and of being mugged. In one dream, Subject X killed Barry and his gang, and I woke up in the morning disappointed it wasn't real.

A few hours later, I sat in my room alone with the darkest music I could find to play. I opened the suitcase and sat crossed-legged on the bed, with the needle in one hand and a sleeve rolled up on the other arm. I had dressed all in black, ready to head out into the night.

I knew where Barry and the gang would be that night, as there was a party being thrown by a sixth form student who was friends with Tony. My music blasted out and the memories of the beating replayed, motivating me to inject the formula and take my revenge. I could kill them all. I could win Scarlett back.

I leant against the bedroom wall, and the bruises ignited in pain. I relived the mugging in my mind; the kicks thumping in, the spit in my face, them shouting offensive threats that rang in my ears, and the tears streaming down my face and it stinging in the cold autumn wind. The memories triggered new tears to roll out my blackened eyes and into my mouth. I relived the stealing of my wallet and phone, and the punch on the nose bursting it open and the blood blending into the tears and saliva. The memories were painful to relive, and my nose bled again, mixing in with my new tears.

My hands tensed up, and I built up my resolve, muscles shaking with anger. I wanted revenge; I wanted them dead. I couldn't go through this again. The formula was the opportunity to fix things. I held my breath and pushed the needle down. The needle depressed the skin on my forearm. The fear of the pain and the feeling of it breaking the skin grew stronger than the desire to keep pushing, so I stopped. I couldn't do it. I was scared of the pain and reaction to the formula. I took long deep breaths, letting my muscles relax.

"Come on, come on," I said to myself.

I tried again, muscles shaking and memories flooding back, and the tears and the blood on my face kept pouring. The needle pushed against the skin, and I felt a scratch as it started to breakthrough.

I stopped again, too scared of the pain. I tried to imagine Subject X and let the memories of the trance force me to do it. I relived the memories of her pacing the room, looking sad with her drooped ashen face, then her transformation into a beautiful goddess with hair flying and red lips, then a vampire snarling with fangs and burning red eyes. In the end, back as a sad, lonely woman again. I felt an affinity for her. The sadness stuck in my mind. We had shared a connection when we first looked at each other.

I realised the mist and the desire were an effect of her powers, and the vampire face a reaction to the UV lights, but the sadness seemed real. I tried to use those memories to inject the needle, but again as soon as the needle depressed against my skin, the fear and pain stopped me. It could kill me and I would die on my bed. I didn't actually know what it would do. I had made an assumption from the psychic images from a vampire and a brief conversation with my Dad. I put the needle back in the suitcase and went back to bed. There must be another way.

I tried to sleep, but only to be met by mashed up dreams of vampires, Scarlett, Barry and the gang.

CHAPTER TEN

When Monday came around again, I reluctantly returned to college. My face still bruised, and I had agreed with Dad to tell everyone I didn't know who had done it.

I wandered to college, with my coat pulled up, and a baseball hat pulled down to hide my bruises and a black eye. I didn't want to go back, but I had to face it. At least they didn't actually go to college unlike back in Leeds. I would be safe inside, and I hoped Scarlett and I could be friends again.

The gang hung around the gates as usual. Barry saw me and nudged a boy with him, and then whispered in his ear. They both glanced over, and the boy jogged across the pavement and thrust my mobile phone into my hands. Maybe my luck had changed. Maybe they wanted to be friends after all.

I walked into the common room and over to the other side, away from Scarlett and Mary. I had said some nasty things to her on Saturday and didn't know what else to do. All the other students looked at my face and whispered to one another. Scarlett looked the other way as I walked in, pretending to be in a deep conversation with Mary.

Then my phone beeped. It was a video with a message. "Play me."

I pressed the button, and the video of my attack began playing on the phone. The video shook about as it showed Tony and John kicking me in the back and legs as I curled up on the floor. They kicked at my head, but my arms and hands covered it up. I watched the close-up of my sad pathetic battered face covered in blood, spit, and tears.

Next, I saw Tony stealing my wallet, phone, and keys. I realised how I lost my keys and felt relief Dad had changed the locks straight away. Watching the video replayed the whole sickening episode again in my mind, and I experienced it from the outside and from within at the same time. My stomach rolled over and I wanted to throw up. The bruises on my back stung as if they had been poked by the memory.

The other phones beeped in the room. In a few seconds, half a dozen phones were playing the sounds of my attack. The muffled noises of screams and laughter in unsynchronised waves of sound echoed around the common room. Those watching it looked over, and a few laughed and handed it around the class. The boys who Scarlett snubbed on the first day laughed the loudest and pointed over at me. They were friends of the gang, and I guessed they were involved in the attack, asking Barry to scare me away. They were enjoying my pain. I went red with anger and humiliation.

I jumped out of my seat, clattering it to the floor, and I banged into people as I ran to the toilets. The laughter followed me down the hallway as I hid in the cubicle, waiting for the bell. I tried to focus on my anger, rather than let my pain take over and the tears to flood. I should have guessed they would send the video about. My phone beeped again, and I had text messages.

"Told you I would make you famous."

"You are such a wimp."

"She won't fancy you now."

The first bell rang, and it triggered my tears to flood out. I wanted revenge on the gang and all those people in the classroom. All those people who happily joined in with the bullies' games. I still had the needles, and maybe I would kill them all. I pictured myself looking like Subject X, a vampire, and wading back into that classroom, tearing their stupid laughing faces apart, ripping them limb from limb and smearing their blood on the walls. They wouldn't be laughing then.

However, I wasn't a violent person. I had never intentionally hurt anyone, and that was why I struggled to take the injection the other night. I was a coward and didn't possess the strength to take the risk of injecting the formula and exacting my revenge.

I stayed in the cubicle trying to work out what to do next. I couldn't sit on the toilet all day and plucked up the courage to face my tormentors. The physics' class had already started, and I stared at the floor as I strode past Scarlett to the back of the room.

The text messages kept coming all day from different numbers. At lunch break, other people at the school huddled around phones, watching the video of my attack, then looking over at me, pointing and laughing. It spread around the college and school like a virus, and anyone with a phone seemed to be watching it or had watched it. I logged on to my new social networking page to be confronted with insults and humiliating comments smeared across it. There was no escape.

People I'd never spoken to before barged, laughed and shouted at me.

"Welcome to London, new boy," one of them shouted.

"Why don't you f off back north, new boy."

"Loser, loser," a group of younger kids from the school chanted at me during the break times and then ran off.

By the afternoon break, I couldn't face people's gazes and bullying, so I hid out of sight. Scarlett and Mary found me hiding out in the art room, in amongst the paints and paper, away from all the crowds and potential bullies. Thoughts of using the needle kept coming back to the forefront of my mind.

I hunched over the desk, frantically scribbling on a piece of paper in a trance of anger and fear.

Revenge, revenge, revenge. I had written again and again on a piece of paper in ever-decreasing circles from the outside towards the centre. In the middle of the paper, I had drawn a picture of Subject X, as I had remembered her that night, flowing hair and seducing red lips, and a hand, offering me one of the red needles.

Scarlett took tentative steps over, and I felt relieved and happy that she still wanted to talk with me. I needed a friend.

"Scarlett, I am so sorry," I blurted out before any stupid ideas stopped me from apologising.

"I know, you were just angry," she replied, walking over and sat beside me, placing a comforting arm around my shoulders.

I leant into her body, put my arms around her and felt comforted by her warmth. Maybe it would be okay after all, as long as I had someone who cared for me and was willing to stand by me. I never did for Giles, but Scarlett might for me. I felt terribly guilty for what had happened to Giles and his family.

My phone beeped again and a picture message arrived. Intrigued, I opened it up. It took a while to work it out, but I could make out red hair, some flesh and numerous bare limbs entwined. My brain finally made sense of the images, and I saw a picture of Scarlett lying beneath Barry. Both semi-naked, with Barry turned towards the camera grinning, and Scarlett flat on her back expressionless. A message came with the photo.

"I told you she was one of ours."

I sat up and thrust the phone into her lap.

"What's this?"

She stared at the picture for an age, and then her body recoiled as the moment of recognition took place. Mary grabbed the phone from her, deleted it quickly and put the phone down on the table.

"What is it?" I asked again, already fearing the answer.

"It was an accident. I met them at the party on Saturday night."

"Oh, he just fell on you."

"No, I was angry with you. I got drunk, and I went over to have a go at them. But he was nice. They told me they thought you were someone else. They never meant it to go so far. If only you hadn't hit them and run away," she said. "I must have had too much to drink to build up the courage. I don't remember much else."

"So you slept with him," I stated bluntly, the anger in me growing every second.

Scarlett got up and walked away, avoiding eye contact.

"Sorry, I never meant to. It just sort of happened. I don't really remember."

"Bitch," I shouted, jumping up, thrusting the chair to the floor and pushing her hard in the back.

Scarlett stumbled forward, her head whipped back, and feet tripped over one another. She crashed forward and bashed her face into the wall. She crumpled onto the floor, and her hands grabbed her nose. Mary rushed over and put her arm around her. Scarlett turned around, and a trickle of blood ran out from beneath her hands and stained her lips red.

"You bastard," Mary screamed.

Scarlett looked at me in horror, tears in her beautiful light green eyes welled up, and then they burst out rolling down her face. Tears of pain and anger? They would have been easier to cope with. The look on her face. I couldn't work it out. Was it surprise? Shock! No, her eyes glazed over and mouth rolled down; it was heartbreak.

Mary lifted Scarlett to her feet and helped her out of the room. They didn't look back. Scarlett was sobbing, and Mary was offering words of comfort as she helped her weave through the tables and chairs out of the room.

"I'm sorry," I shouted in vain, but it was pointless.

Maybe I was a violent person after all, and I sat alone to confront the rest of the nightmare by myself.

I stared back down at the picture I had been drawing of Subject X while trying to think of what to do next. The words revenge circling her started spinning anti-clockwise around the outside of the picture, going faster and faster until they merged in a blur of spinning letters. Then the hand holding the needle rose out of the page, offering its solution. I blinked a few times to shake it off. No effect. The picture of her smiled, then bared razor sharp fangs, and her eyes flickered to a fiery red. I shook my head and stared back again. The picture had returned to normal.

I only had one option left to end my torment.

CHAPTER ELEVEN

Anger consumed my every thought. I'd lost everything and realised what I'd done to Giles, not just on that day, but all those days afterwards when I didn't talk to him. I had tried to justify it all this time that I had done the right thing, looked away on that day and looked away every day afterwards as well. My mind raged, and images of Subject X flooded back.

"Blood and anger," she had spoken into my mind.

I remembered the image of her in a terrifying, beautiful vampiric rage, smashing at the mirror that separated us, with blood red eyes, contorting muscles and snarling fangs. My mind was made up. I had nowhere else to turn. No one else who could help. I didn't want to be scared anymore, and I didn't want to be a victim anymore. Things had to change. The formula would either kill me or offer me vengeance. I didn't want to end up like Giles lying in a warm bath with blood pouring from my wrists. At least by taking the formula, it would give me a chance. Either way, this would end tonight.

I knew the gang hung out at a park in the centre of town. Scarlett and Mary had told me to avoid it at night. After what had happened with Scarlett, I left college early and ran home to prepare myself. I removed the needle from the suitcase, placed it on top of my stereo, and turned on some loud and dark music.

The needle vibrated as the bass shook the room, and I grabbed a change of clothes from my wardrobe. I took off the clothes I had recently bought when I tried to be more like Scarlett. When I tried to fit in with the crowd by being more fashionable. I dragged out from the corner of the wardrobe, the dark and dingy clothes I had worn on that first day at college. I had returned to being the same person when I had arrived in London, wearing dirty frayed and ripped jeans, army boots, black t-shirt, and an old beaten up black leather jacket. Then I realised I was actually better off as the person on the first day of college. Life was much worse now that I had found Scarlett and been betrayed by her, and viciously beaten, humiliated and bullied at college.

The music blared out into my room, and the song, "Charlotte the Harlot," came on. I sang along changing the words to, "Scarlett the Harlot."

It started to get dark. I turned the music off, slipped the needle into my pocket and stormed downstairs. I slapped some peanut butter in between two slices of bread as the sunlight faded through the kitchen window. I slipped out to the park, occasionally feeling my pocket for the needle and munching on the makeshift sandwich.

The park resided on the edge of a rough area, and I could get into problems just being there, let alone looking for trouble. I walked along the pavement at the side of the road that ran along the edge of the park and found a tree to hide behind. I leant behind it, taking glimpses of them in the playground area.

Scattered around the park, I saw their bikes and skateboards they had dumped on arrival. The playground area was situated right at the back, next to a pocket of trees, and a fence ran all the way down the back. Houses on either side of the park enclosed it in, with just the route across the grass to the pavement and road as the only way in and out.

Their dark hooded figures wandered about as the car headlights occasionally lit them up. They sprawled out around the playground equipment. Two on the swings, one sat at the bottom of the slide, two on the table facing the swings, and one walking about and talking on his mobile phone. They occasionally got up, passed around the drinks and smokes, threw empty cans against the railings and flicked out cigarettes onto the grass. Their faces lit up from using their phones, and the beeping of text messages bounced about to one another.

Barry sat on the swings, rocking back and forth, as he dragged on a cigarette, and his mountain bike leant against the playground railings. The others congregated around him and deferred to his presence, making it easy to spot him. They were all there and most importantly, the ones who attacked me: Barry, John and Tony.

All the time, my hand rolled the needle up and down my palm. I only had to plunge it into my arm, and I might have my revenge. I could storm across that park with fangs snarling, ready to rip their bodies apart.

Yet, I still couldn't do it. I had always looked the other way and hid from trouble. Anger and rage had forced me here, but in the cold night air and the sight of the brutal gang members, my real nature took over. I was a coward. The truth was the fear of it killing me held me back. I didn't know for sure what would happen if I took the injection. It might not even be the formula but some other drug. Even if it did work, was I ready to be a murderer?

Just then, Barry finished his cigarette and jumped over the railing onto his bike. He cycled out of the park, and I dipped behind the tree. I turned back and watched for a couple more minutes, hoping he would return, and then my phone beeped.

"Call her," the message read from Mary.

I wanted to apologise for hurting Scarlett, but the image of her with Barry still burnt my eyes. Every time I closed them, it stared back at me taunting and laughing. It was worse than the mugging. The bruises were healing, but her betrayal would never leave me. I realised how Giles felt about me when I betrayed him. Even if I could speak to him now, I doubt he would want to talk.

I looked up from the phone, and Tony and John started heading towards me. Those two again. Tony with his long stride as his clothes flapped about unable to cling to his slight frame. John walked with intent and his face scowled as he pumped his large muscles onwards. Time to go. Maybe in a few days, I could forget what Scarlett had done and try to rebuild our relationship. I could forgive her, and I hoped one day Giles would forgive me. I would hand the needles back to Dad and try to forget ever seeing the beautiful vampire.

I turned to walk off, but I walked straight into someone standing behind me. Barry's big face grinned as he head-butted me on my bruised nose. I clutched my hands up to protect it as fresh blood ran out, and I staggered back from the pain. Hands grabbed at my arms, twisting them around my back and turning the wrists over themselves. Pain shot through my arms and Tony and John manhandled me around, and frog marched me back to the playground area where the rest of the gang eagerly awaited.

Why did I come here? I should have known it would go wrong. Why couldn't I just take the injection and have my revenge?

Barry followed on, occasionally smacking the back of my head.

"Watching us, boy, do you want more? I have got some plans for you if you enjoy making films."

Tony and John threw me into the waiting clutches of the rest of the gang.

"Tie him," Barry commanded.

They pushed me down onto the floor, in amongst the cigarette ends and empty drinks cans, and pushed my back onto the metal fence railings. They used their belts to tie my arms to the fence. I felt the damp floor soaking into my trousers; it stunk of beer and urine. I felt nauseous, wet and scared. It was going to be another beating but even worse than before.

Barry walked in front of me, crouched down, and looked me straight in the eye.

"What do you think you're up to?" he asked, slapping me around the side of the head.

The rest of the gang laughed like a pack.

"Why you here?" he asked and punched my chest. The air burst out, leaving me breathless.

"I don't know," I said, not able to give an actual answer.

"Consequences, new boy. You date my girlfriend and hang about watching me, and then things get worse."

He punched again.

"Scarlett was fun. Isn't that right, boys?"

The gang laughed again, making vulgar gestures with imaginary women.

"Check him."

Andy rummaged through my pockets, throwing its contents in front of me: wallet, phone, keys and needle. They grabbed some of the stuff each and Barry picked up the needle.

"What the hell is this for?"

I just looked at him, not sure what to say. Barry nodded at Andy, and he punched me in the face, and my head banged off the railings.

"What ... is ... it ... for," Barry said again, but slowly this time as if I didn't understand the question.

In my bruised and dazed state, I said the first thing that came to mind.

"Diabetes," I slurred out of my damaged mouth as my head spun.

Barry threw it to the floor and went to stamp on it.

"NO," I shouted, clinging on to my only hope of surviving this ordeal.

Barry laughed. "Why?"

"If I don't get my injection, I could die."

Barry paused with his foot above the needle.

"It would be murder. That's a big step," I said.

Barry stopped grinning, put his foot back down away from the needle, picked it up and walked over.

The next words just blurted out.

"I need to take it in two hours, not now. It would work but would make me feel sick."

"Like what."

"Stomach ache and loss of bodily control," I added for extra effect, appealing to his nasty side.

"What, wet yourself?" he laughed.

"Eeer, no, no," I looked away with my best acting.

"You do, don't you? Well, get ready, here comes the doctor," he said, kneeling in front of me while the others pulled up the sleeve of my coat and shirt.

I suddenly changed my mind, scared of the consequences either way. Death by unknown formula or turning into a murderous vampire. I shouted at them to stop.

"No, no, please don't do it, you will regret it," I shouted, but they laughed, not understanding my protests were for their own protection.

Barry stabbed the needle in without ceremony and then pushed the formula into my bloodstream. He stood up and stepped back with his hand clutched around his phone, ready to film again.

The fluid mixed in with my blood and explosions fired through my body. My muscles shook and flesh contorted as they spasmed into their new alignment. My heart raced, trying to keep the blood flowing into my altering body, feeding it the fuel to change.

The puncture mark on my arm shrivelled away, and the flesh glowed red with a burning heat that flooded through my body. I shook violently, making it look like I was having a fit. The gang started laughing again, and Barry's face erupted into a malicious grin, excited to be capturing it for future enjoyment.

My heart thumped harder and harder into my chest. I sucked in the air, trying to pump the oxygen into my muscles as they struggled to hold their shape. I couldn't hold it together, as the momentum tore my muscles and flesh apart. Pain seared through my limbs, and I strained at my bonds, muscles tensing and gushing red with blood as it carried the catalyst of the formula.

I started hyperventilating, desperate to ride out each surge of pain and fear. But my heart seized, spasmed and pain shot down my left-hand side. My chest felt like it was collapsing and crushing my heart. Finally, my heart imploded under the pressure.

I screamed as the burning flesh and heart attack took their toll, and everything went dark. My eyelids dropped shut. My senses shut down, and I drifted off into a silent black world. Peace at last. The formula had solved my problems. I was dead. I didn't feel pain anymore or had to worry about revenge or love. At last, it was all over.

But it didn't last. My heart hit back stronger, and my lungs burst back to life. I sucked in massive gulps of air, bringing my oxygen levels back to normal, refuelling my body. My eyes remained closed, but I heard many heavy hearts beating around me. My eyelids flashed open, and the gang stared at me. Orange waves glowed around their bodies as a heat silhouette, and a yellow light pulsed from their hearts, flashing like a beacon in the dark.

I narrowed my eyes to focus in the gloom, and the individual spots and hairs on their faces stood out. Andy's face in fresh cuts, with fragments of red nail varnish stuck in them. The smell of cheap aftershave, tobacco and alcohol assaulted my nostrils. Bad breath and body odour poured out from Tony, and chips and cigarettes on Andy.

Their hormones, testosterone I guessed, drifted out from their bodies in the background of the other odours. I sensed excited and violent thoughts in their minds. Hurry up, Barry thought. Images of violence raced across Andy's mind, pictures of his fist in my face. The cold air, the damp grass, and the pain from my bruises had dissipated. I tested the leather bonds around my arms and knew they would break if required.

"Revenge, revenge, my darling," Subject X's strange voice and image returned to me.

Her raven hair billowed in a supernatural wind. Her arms stretched out, and her lips and cheeks flushed a bloodied red. The mist poured out of the wet ground and began swirling around me, sending tingling sparks through my arms and legs, shooting through my spine and firing my desire. The musky smell of the mist washed through my nose, soaking its receptors and triggering my hormones. I felt connected to her again. I wanted to get up and find her so I could embrace her as a vampire.

"Come on, do something, that was boring," Barry shouted and cursed in frustration. "Kick him."

Tony stepped across and snapped a long powerful kick into my stomach.

I snapped out of the trance, and the vampire in me took charge. Everything changed. The pain ignited a supernatural aggression across my whole body. My eyes burnt as they transformed into a fiery red with black splits in the middle. My fangs stabbed through my mouth and pierced the air. I snarled and growled at them from the pit of my stomach. The bass of the low growl resonated through my body and shook the surrounding ground. I knew what they were experiencing, as I had been through it only days before when she launched herself at the glass. Their mouths wide open and bodies transfixed to the spot, unable to comprehend the transformation in front of them while fear drowned their bodies.

The belts and railings tore apart as I freed myself from my leather bondage. I stood up and tensed all my muscles, and I roared a wave of stale air and spit across their faces, forcing them back. Only Barry had the sense to have already run away. The rest were meat.

John sprinted off like a freight train, and Tony ran with his long legs wheeling around as his tracksuit bottoms flapped about. They scattered too quickly to get them all, and I would have to let Barry go and focus on the others.

A trail of yellow light from their increased heartbeats traced across the dark park, and the orange glow around their bodies turned a darker colour, as they heated up from the fear and the sudden burst of energy.

As the adrenaline kicked in for them to take flight, their scents left a unique invisible path, identifying each of my potential victims. Fear consumed their emotions, and I experienced something beyond anger and rage, a primaeval instinct to kill. The images of me as a vampire filled their minds; fangs snarling in the air and eyes raging with blood and fire. I smiled.

I needed to stop them from getting out of the park, and I threw one of the broken railings at Tony as he ran. The metal railing spun and arched around, hitting him on the back of his head, dropping him to the floor. I threw another metal rail at John, and it penetrated through the back of his head. He fell to the floor, with the railing embedded in his skull, pointing skywards. He was dead all too easily.

I picked up Andy's scent next and followed his light path. I tensed my hands and my claws ripped through the ends of my fingers, but I barely registered the pain. I sprinted past him, swinging back with my claws, slicing his throat in one smooth action. The blood sprayed out as he tumbled to the floor, and then he bled out onto the grass.

On to Mike, he had reached the trees and thought he was safe, but the yellow pulse acted like a lighthouse, drawing me closer. I sunk my claws through his well-groomed hair into his skull and yanked back to stop him from running away. I tore his head off his shoulders, with his spinal cord flailing behind it as his body ran on for a few yards under its own momentum. Blood pumped out the top of his body like a fountain as it slumped onto the grass, sliding onwards and staining the ground red around his headless body. I was stronger than I realised.

I dropped his head on the floor as I picked up George's scent heading into the trees at the back of the park. I sniffed the air and followed it through the trees and circled around his back. His fear grew as I closed in, and his heart hammered. His head and eyes flitted about like a meerkat, and he pushed his wiry body into the trees to hide. I approached quick and silent from behind, but he turned in time and stabbed with a knife. The stabbing knife moved in slow motion, and I swiped my fist across, knocking the knife out of his hand. I speared my clawed hand through his throat, seized his windpipe and ripped it out. The blood burst out, splattering my face and chest as he dropped dead to the mud.

It felt fantastic. I was faster, stronger, and more aggressive than ever before. In those thirty seconds, I smashed and tore their limbs apart and scattered them about the park, and they now covered the grass in fresh warm blood. I wiped my hand across my face, gathering up the blood splattered across it and then sucked my fingers dry. The blood tasted coppery in my mouth at first and then sweet as it slipped down the back of my throat. Its energy kicked in, and I shuddered with a renewed strength.

I didn't need to think of what to do, as an animal instinct had taken over. It seemed uncontrollable. I felt no remorse or guilt in killing them, just pure satisfaction. My fears had come true. I had become a murderous vampire. But I didn't care.

The life force in Tony sung to me from across the park, and I blazed across the wet grass as he slowly tried to get up. As he crawled away, the veins on his neck pumped, offering its bounty to me. I wanted more and felt the urge. The image of her again, that beautiful vampire woman, called to me.

"Feed."

I dropped to my knees, grabbed hold of his leg and dragged him backwards. He screamed and kicked in a futile gesture of survival. I parried the kicks and pulled him closer. I wrenched his head back, exposed the sweet spot of his open neck and gave in to my urges. The blood pumped in, filling my vampire body with power and quenching its thirst.

As I fed, her image continued to beckon to me, as it had done in the research centre. He struggled with arms and legs thrashing about and screaming to no effect. I sucked harder, draining his body of life.

"Good boy. Now come to me." Her voice sounded stronger and more urgent than ever after the killing. I had to see her again.

CHAPTER TWELVE

Nothing happened on the journey to the research centre. I pulled my coat closed to conceal the blood on my shirt, and I dropped my eyes to the ground so no one could see their mutation. Once on the major roads, I ran as fast as my new power would let me. I wanted to get back before my vampire power ran out. By the time I arrived, I had gained control of the mutation and wiped the blood off my face, so I appeared normal to the security guards at the gates.

The guard remembered me and nodded as I approached.

"Need to call my Dad again," I said.

He dialled through and handed the phone over.

"Who is it?" Dad said.

"It's me, Jonathan, I need to come in."

"Why?"

"I have been in another fight."

"They beat you up again?" he asked.

I couldn't answer properly with the guard listening.

"No, the other way round."

There was a long pause.

"Did you take the needles?" Dad asked.

"Yes."

"Wait there," he responded, and the phone went dead.

He came to the front gates dressed in his standard lab coat and black trousers, and he signed me through. We hurried through the main white marble lobby, around the desk, through to the corridor directly behind it, and down the endless white corridors to the lift. As soon as I entered the base, Subject X started calling to me.

'Welcome back, my darling...Come to me now.'

The image of her as a beautiful goddess, raven hair flowing and sky bright eyes dazzling, replayed over and over again in my mind. I could feel her ghostly tentacles sweeping desire across my body, but I found, with my new powers, I could resist if I wanted.

We got into the lift.

"So what happened tonight?" Dad asked.

"I went to the park the gang hung out in and took a needle with me."

"You took the injection and killed them," he said, staring at the lift doors the whole time.

"They caught me and found the needle. I told them I was diabetic, so

The Birth of Vengeance

they wouldn't break the needle. Then I tricked them into injecting me."

"How?"

"I said I needed it later, but not now as it would affect my bodily functions."

"Oh. So they thought it would be funny to make you ill."

"Yes. But I had the last laugh."

My Dad paused for a moment, looked at me wide-eyed, and smiled. "Tell me about the transformation."

"For the transformation to work, it had to kill me first. But I was snapped back to life."

"Okay. Then what? What is it like being a vampire?"

"Well. The transformation hurts. My body felt like it was ripped apart and put back together again. Afterwards, my sight, hearing, and smell had all improved." I sniffed the air. "You've been drinking and had pepperoni pizza."

"It was Gabriel's, my boss, birthday party. Just a cold buffet and a few cans of lager. I only had half a can. It's nothing to worry about."

"Obviously, my strength and speed improved. The gang fled as I transformed and ripped out of the straps they had used to tie me to the metal railings. With my improved senses, I tracked them down and killed them," I said.

"But how did you kill them?"

'Yes, tell us.' Subject X's voice chimed into my thoughts again.

"I killed one by throwing a metal railing through his skull. The next by slashing his throat. One by tearing his head off his shoulders. Another one had a knife, but I disarmed him and then ripped out his windpipe. The last one I drained of blood."

'Hmm. Delicious. I can see it all now we are connected again. I can relive every moment. I loved the way you ripped his head off.'

"You drank blood. Why?" Dad asked.

"Instinct. The blood gave me extra strength."

"Did it? I wondered what would happen. So you killed them all?"

"No. The gang leader escaped. He filmed the transformation as well. I still want him dead."

"Oh. This is bad news. We can't let that film be published. I need to get it off him to stop it going viral. Plus, it would be good to see the transformation for my research. Give me the name and Gabriel will arrange for it to be retrieved."

"How?"

"Easily. I work for a military research agency. They will send around the army."

"Oh. But you couldn't have arranged for them to go around after I had been attacked?"

"No. They wouldn't get involved in something like that. That is a domestic issue."

We walked into the basement, and two security guards approached us carrying their guns.

"He isn't allowed down here, Sir," they bellowed out as we walked in.

Instinct took over, and I flashed across to them. I punched one in the jaw, and he crashed to the floor. The other swung around his rifle, but I pushed it away and kicked him in the groin. He dropped to his knees, clutching himself. I whipped in a left hook, knocking him out. I kicked open the office door next to my Dad's, and then dragged them through and cuffed them to the radiator.

I walked back to the corridor where my Dad stood frozen to the spot staring at me.

"What?" I asked.

"That was amazing," he said.

"Dad, what did you expect?"

He just shrugged his shoulders and ushered me into his room with the tinted mirror. I dropped into the seat, and he pulled out some empty needles from the cupboard.

"What are you doing?" I asked.

"Samples, you are our first test case."

"I am not a test case. I am your son."

Once I sat down, I noticed ten more red needles lined up on the side.

"How many of these needles have you made?" I asked, pointing at them.

"That's it after you took the last ones, which was our first batch. This is our latest run. We need to test them, but I guess you have done that for us."

He came at me again with the empty needle, looking for samples.

"Give me your arm, Jonathan."

I backed off as he approached.

"No. This research is wrong, Dad. She is wrong. It can't be allowed to continue."

He looked surprised. "Why?"

"I killed people tonight, Dad, without remorse, without any thought. It was too easy. This research has to be destroyed. We have to kill her," I shouted and pointed at the mirror.

Subject X's voice in my head stopped. Dad looked dumbfounded.

"It's the only way," I said again.

"No, this is my work, you can't!"

"I can and I will. This isn't up for debate. Now leave," I said.

"No," he responded, stood upright and looked down at me, exerting all of his years of fatherhood.

"Go," I screamed and snarled at him with my best vampire face.

His face faltered from authority to fear. His eyebrows recoiled upwards, eyes stretched wide, and his mouth pulled back. He rushed out of the room and headed straight for the lift. I ran past him and blocked his path.

"No alarms, just leave," I said, staring straight into his eyes.

He nodded his head and jumped into the waiting lift. I walked back to the security guards and took a gun and a card pass for the prison cell. The gun had two settings, human and vampire. I switched it to vampire and walked to the cell door. Her voice in my head remained silent.

I opened the cell door and levelled the gun at the ready. She didn't hide. She stood in the middle of the room, naked and smiling. I smiled at her and took a cautious step inside. Her tousled raven hair started flickering, her lips a lustful red and body glistening with warmth.

"My darling, you have returned to me," she said in a soft voice.

"You know what I want," I said, pulling the gun up to my eye to take aim.

"Yes," she said, smiled and stretched her arms out, "you are here for your reward."

The vampire formula in my bloodstream remained too strong for her psychic abilities, but I still lowered the gun and dropped it clattering to the floor.

"Yes," I said, voice shaking, allowing my real emotions to become apparent.

"I will make you a proper vampire one day, but first, I shall make you a man."

She sauntered over, giving me time to soak in her beauty and then stood face-to-face with me. She leant forward, her seductive red lips millimetres away from mine, her sky eyes dazzling and the heat from her body warming my face. Her hand glided down my arm, sending a tingling sensation racing up it, and I breathed in sharply, trying to control myself. Her fingers slid across the palm of my hand and cradled it. She turned and led me back to her bed. I followed on without thinking. My heart thumped and the heat of my desire ignited.

"I will take care of everything," she whispered in my ear as she laid me down on her bed.

She straddled over me and pulled down my trousers. She then grabbed my hands and placed them onto her warm glistening body.

"Relax and enjoy," she said, and began gyrating and writhing around on top of me.

I ran my hands all over her firm, hot body. Her heat surprised me, as I expected her to be icy cold, but it wasn't just warm, it was hotter than it should be. The heat electrified my skin, and it seeped into my body as I touched her. This wasn't how I imagined my first time. I didn't imagine it would be in a prison cell with a vampire, just after I had killed five people. I had hoped it would have been a romantic night with Scarlett.

I looked up at Subject X, her tousled dark hair flowing backwards again. Her cheeks flushed, and her lips were full and bloody red. The mist poured around the room as she writhed on top of me, with her hair blowing, body arching, and a soft moaning purring out of her. Time froze as I abandoned myself to her pleasure.

She moved faster and with more vigour, picking up the speed and power with every thrust, her body boiling like a furnace. She slowed down, closing her eyes, clenching her mouth shut, and I felt a shudder running through her and my moment had arrived. I tensed up, and her eyes opened, changing to blood red, and fangs appeared as she sucked in the air. I tried to sink back into the bed to escape, but she bolted down at me, moving my head to one side and bit into my neck. Her body pumped from fangs to hips as she started draining me, and I experienced pleasure and pain at the same time.

She didn't take much and sat back up, looking down at me with blood running from her fangs. Blood dripped off her chin and ran down her chest, taking the path of least resistance, channelling into the valley between her breasts. The mist and the breeze disappeared, and her face changed back to normal apart from the blood dripping from her chin, which soaked in leaving no trace. The blood on her chest absorbed behind the line running down to her naval. The blood trails left her skin clean and glowing.

"Enjoy, darling?"

"Yes, but I thought you were going to kill me."

"No, not yet. When it's time for you to become a proper vampire. I need to make you a man first."

She jumped off and pulled on her black combat trousers and vest top.

"I'm not a man now?"

"Ha ha, it's more than just making love. You will find out."

I sat there in silence for a moment, thinking about what to do next. I swung out of bed and pulled my trousers back up.

"What is your name?" I asked.

"Thorn."

"Thorn?"

"If you touch me, you bleed," she said, smiled and winked. "Your name?"

"Jonathan Harper."

"Hello, Jonathan Harper. I am pleased to meet you."

I stood up and looked in the mirror, realising that all the bruises around my face had disappeared. I also felt strange and looked a little different. My clothes clung tighter than before. The gap between the end of my trousers and shoes had grown, and my toes squashed into the ends. I studied my reflection more closely. I had grown bigger and stronger, and I guessed it was a residual effect of the formula. But at some point since arriving, the formula had worn off. I had returned to plain human again, and with it, uncertainty about my decisions crept in.

"We leave now," she said and headed through the door.

I ran after her.

"Where are we going?" I asked.

"Take the needles and destroy the research," she said.

I didn't question and shoved the needles into a bag, and then sprayed the equipment with the machine gun, ripping through it and causing glass and metal to fly. Thorn found some combustible fluid and poured it all over the lab and the surrounding offices. I realised what she intended to do.

"The guards?" I asked.

"And?" she responded.

"We must take them out," I pleaded with her, not wanting any more blood on my hands that night.

"Okay, this time, but you will learn," she answered, annoyed at my interruption.

She flung the guards over her shoulders, and I threw a lighted match into the lab and we left.

As we got into the lift, the fire caught, and the flames danced around the edges of the doorframe from my father's office.

We reached the top and the lift doors opened, and Thorn threw the two guards on her shoulders into the paths of an oncoming posse of soldiers. They tumbled to the floor, allowing Thorn to jump through the gap, and punch and kick those trying to regain their feet. She knocked them down and out. Blood broke across their faces and spat out their mouths as the force of her blows connected with their feeble human bodies. I followed on with my gun aimed at their faces, keeping them flat against the floors and walls.

We sprinted down the hallways, flicking the access pass at the security readers to open them, and I pointed the gun back to stop the guards. The halls rang with the sounds of the fire alarms, and the red lights flashed on the walls.

At the main lobby, a group of five guards waited behind the desk, guns levelled and aimed as we arrived. The lobby had two big glass doors at the front and an enclosed desk area in the middle where the receptionist usually sat.

"Follow my instructions," she shouted.

She grabbed the back of my jacket and slid me along the floor behind the enclosed desk. She skidded along beside me on her stomach, taking cover. A flurry of bullets bounced down the corridor behind us, as the guards tried to halt our escape.

'Shoot the lights,' she said into my mind, along with the image of the lights above the guards. I leant back, arched the gun over the top of the desk area, aimed up and fired off the bullets in a reckless spray, causing the lobby to descend into darkness, and the metal and glass above the guard's heads to rain down.

'Stop,' she said in my mind.

The guards covered their heads and eyes. Thorn crouched back a few steps and leapt over the desk and into the raining sparks of metal and glass. The crack of bones and screams pierced the air between the sounds of the falling debris showering like hailstones across the white marble lobby floor.

'Out,' she shouted into my mind, and I bolted around the side, jumping across bodies of broken men and out into the night.

Lights flashed and alarms wailed, and guards in army uniforms emerged, swarming in from every direction as spotlights swung around, trying to highlight us.

"Hunters!" Thorn shouted and pulled me to the ground.

Two men dressed in grey combat overalls and black army boots ran at us with rifles pointed in our direction. One of them stopped and threw something from his hand.

"UV grenade. Shoot them," she shouted.

Thorn ran around the corner, and I fired the machine gun. The bullets fired aimlessly, but it slowed them down and forced them to take cover behind walls and pillars, which formed the entrance shelter at the front of the building. The grenade landed next to me, and UV light sparked out in a huge sphere lighting up the entire area.

I looked around for Thorn, but she had already escaped. I shot at the light, trying to hide our position and protect Thorn from the harmful rays, but I missed. I received images and a message from Thorn: gun into your shoulder, look down the barrel and through the target point, brace for impact and fire in bursts. The light exploded as the bullets impacted and we returned to the safety of darkness.

The bullets from the Hunters rained over my head, and I fired back following the instructions from Thorn. I stood and fired in bursts. Behind them, a dark shape dropped from the roof and ran at them, sweeping the first one off his feet and sending the Hunter flying. The other one turned from seeing his partner flying overhead but was too late as Thorn clotheslined him in a blur of legs and arms.

The last Hunter catapulted backwards, slammed into the side of the building and bounced, leaving a splattering of blood marking the impact. The first guard landed across the barbed wire electric fence. His body shook as the electricity found a circuit through his body, causing smoke to rise from his flesh. The spasming muscles in his fingers pulled the trigger and bullets fired off in wild bursts across the campus. The other guards dived for cover from their unknown assailant.

I turned back as she lifted me up and swung me onto her shoulders without stopping. We darted off around the corner to the back of the building and away from the remaining guards that were closing in on our position. There was no escape as we ran along by the high fence. We were trapped.

She curved back towards the building and ran up the wall to the first floor. When the momentum caught up with us, she crouched and rocketed up and outwards over the fence, arching over and back flipping into an empty field. She executed a perfect landing and ran into her stride.

Thorn ran off into the darkness with me still on her shoulders. She ran quicker carrying me than I could have run alongside her. After about ten minutes, police and fire engine sirens broke through the quiet night, and the noise of a helicopter buzzed in the distance. Thorn ran down a dark alley on the first housing estate we came to and dropped me to the ground.

"They will come for us," she said, looking up into the sky towards the sound of the helicopter. "Probably made up some random crime to use the police to capture us."

"What do we do?" I asked.

"What time is it?"

I had lost track of time altogether and looked down at my watch.

"It's 10 pm."

"We need to hide out for a bit 'til tomorrow night. I doubt we can make it all the way to my house before daylight with the police hunting us down. Plus, I am tired. They kept me near starvation point as a way of keeping me subdued. That's why I took some of your blood," she said.

She closed her eyes and stood motionless for a few seconds.

"They have dogs tracking us. We need to shake them off and find somewhere to hide. Can you swim?" she asked.

"Yes."

She darted off through the alleyway, and I followed her.

We snaked through alleys and streets, all the time the helicopter drew nearer, and the police sirens wailed with the odd flash of blue lights cutting through the night.

We made it to a canal, and Thorn waited for me at the edge.

"We swim for a bit to lose the scent and cool our bodies down," she said.

I looked at her puzzled.

"I burn a little hotter than normal people. They could detect me," she said.

She jumped in and swam effortlessly down the canal and out the other side.

I jumped in. The cold water shocked me to a stand still for a few seconds, and I front crawled in a panic down the canal towards Thorn. The water dragged me down in my leather coat, and the water shot up my nose and down into the back of my mouth. I coughed and spluttered, forcing my arms and legs onwards, keeping Thorn in view as my motivation. I made it. She grabbed my hand and lifted me straight out of the water and onto my feet. I stood shivering, wondering if I could carry on as my body started shutting down.

"You will be okay," she said, hugging me as she leant towards my ear.

"We will find somewhere warm and get you out of those wet clothes," she said in a mischievous tone.

She grabbed my hand and ran, pulling me along behind her. I slapped the ground with my wet feet, warming me up and squishing the water out of my clothes and shoes. We ran across a cricket pitch and towards more houses, avoiding the nearby town centre because of the CCTV cameras.

We ran for another ten minutes, but I lagged with the cold taking its toll and my body exhausted from the vampire transformation. We ran across a golf course, and Thorn stopped next to a bunker as I staggered forward to keep up.

"Rest for a second," she said and closed her eyes, reaching out with her senses once again.

The helicopter sounded close, and the police cars dashed about nearby roads. She opened her eyes and looked into the sky in the helicopter's direction.

"They will be here soon. Strip," she said.

She flung her clothes to the floor, and I followed on, fingers shaking and numb, struggling to coordinate the movements needed to unzip my jacket and pull my jeans down. Thorn had stripped to her underwear and rushed over to pull off the last of my clothes.

"Any excuse to get me to undress you?" she joked.

She grabbed my clothes, shoved them on the floor, and lay down on top of them, face up.

"Come on, get on top," she said.

I lay on top of her as the helicopter flew overhead.

She rubbed her hands down my back.

"Our bodies together and our coldness with cover my additional heat signature. I doubt they will think it is us. Let's hope they think it's just two young lovers."

The helicopter hovered for a while, and I guessed they enjoyed the sight. Trees and bushes down the side of the golf course rippled under the waves of air being blasted down upon us. Sand swirled about in the bunker, covering us in a light dusting, and I shut my eyes as it blew across my face.

Her body started warming up, and I readily absorbed the heat. Waves of air forced the cold water off my body and flapped our hair about and dried it off. A spotlight came on, and Thorn grabbed my head and covered her face into my chest, pretending to hide as a person caught in the act would. I held still, hoping to copy her pretend embarrassment of being watched. The helicopter hovered. Eventually, the blasted air ceased, and the sound of the buzzing blades disappeared.

She pushed me off and flung my clothes at me. She grabbed her clothes, wrung them dry, and I copied. I watched her body in the moonlight as she pulled the vest top back on over her wet swept back hair. I still found it hard to comprehend the truth that she was a vampire, and I was her rescuer and lover.

I fought with the wet clothes in the dark, trying to get them back on. Luckily, the skin-to-skin contact with Thorn had warmed me up, and I had enough feelings in my hands to force them on.

With our clothes back on, Thorn picked me up again and ran across the golf course into another housing estate. She stopped still and closed her eyes again.

"The house on the corner is empty. We can get in from the back of the golf course. I will check it over," she said.

We ran around to a high fence at the back. Thorn scaled over it and broke into the house. I shivered while scouting around for anyone watching. She dropped back over the fence and scooped me up. She ran up the fence and over the other side, straight into the house and dumped me onto a sofa.

"We should be safe here," she said.

"How do you know?" I asked.

"No one has been in this house for a few days. I can sense it. There are no cars outside, and the calendar on the fridge says they are returning from holiday next Saturday."

"Oh."

"We both need to rest. Tomorrow night, I will get us both some food and new clothes. We will go to my house the night after that. The search will have gone cold, and we can scout out the surroundings properly. No need to rush. We have time to get back safely. Now let's get you out of those wet clothes properly this time," she said and pulled me off the sofa and up the stairs. She turned on a hot shower, and we both stripped off and climbed in together.

The hot water relieved the cold, and as I stood in the shower, Thorn massaged shower gel onto my body and washed it off. Pleasure and warmth flowed through my body, and my thoughts turned away from running and fear to the fun I might have with Thorn. I repaid the favour, and I enjoyed every moment my hands touched her perfect body. Enjoying her turn, she closed her eyes and leant against the shower wall as I washed her clean. Her usual high heat flooded back to her body, seeping into my hands from our contact.

We dried off and found some clothes to wear while ours dried out. Thorn opened the loft hatch and pulled down a ladder.

"We sleep up here, out of sight and sound from any potential visitors and safe from the sunlight," she said.

We grabbed a couple of single mattresses and some blankets, dragged them through the hatch and set up a bed for the next couple of days.

In the dark and finally safe, I realised everything had changed. I had killed the gang and freed a vampire. I couldn't go home. My life or death belonged to Thorn.

CHAPTER THIRTEEN

I fell asleep in moments with the activities of the night before having taken their toll, and Thorn held me in her arms for most of the day while she slept. I couldn't decide if she did this to prevent me from escaping, or for the enjoyment of my company after being imprisoned alone. Either way, I slept happily next to her and felt safe with her by my side while her heat kept me warm and comfortable all day. As the night fell, I woke up to see Thorn crouched next to the loft hatch.

"I will return," she said before disappearing off through the hole in the floor.

I scouted around the house and found some food. I found a torch and a book, and went to read in the loft, but I couldn't focus. Instead, I just lay in the semi-darkness wondering what would happen next, realising what I had just done. I had killed five people and helped a vampire escape her prison, and now I was on the run with her. Now alone, I thought about what had happened, and I realised what a monumental mess I had landed myself in. I had my revenge, except for Barry, but at what cost? Eventually, she would kill me, and if she didn't kill me straight away, she would turn me into a vampire instead.

At the time of breaking her out of prison, it seemed an excellent idea, but the influence of the vampire formula had clouded my judgement. I wasn't sure I wanted to be a vampire. I enjoyed the rush and the revenge on the gang, but life as a vampire would be something different. It would be an eternity of killing people for food and living in the dark. I needed to think of a way out. I could leave right now and run away into the night, but she would probably find me. The UV could stop her from following me, so daylight would provide the best opportunity. For the moment, I just waited for her return, hoping she wouldn't come back, and I would be free.

An hour before sunlight, the hatch door opened up. It startled me, as I would have expected to hear some noise of her re-entering the house first. Her head popped through the hole, and she displayed a satisfied grin.

"Food and clothes for you," she said and threw a bag containing a burger and chips, and then threw another plastic bag containing new clothes to replace my blood-covered ones.

"I will have a shower. You eat and then your turn," she said and disappeared back through the hatch. I tore open the bag and devoured the food.

On her return, I tried not to think about escaping, knowing she could read my mind. Instead, I thought about anything else, like re-enacting scenes from Star Wars movies in my mind, so she couldn't detect my real thoughts and emotions.

When Thorn came back, we swapped over and I showered, changed and rejoined her in the loft. The whole time I showered and changed, I worried about what she would do next.

"Come here, my darling," she said as I re-entered the loft.

Thorn lay down on the mattress and beckoned me over. I walked over and lay down next to her, face-to-face. We stared into each other's eyes. My wet hair dropped across my face, shielding me from her gaze. She brushed it away with one hand and then placed her hand on my cheek.

"My saviour," she said and gave me a sweet smile.

She moved towards me and placed a light kiss on my lips and smiled again.

"We sleep now. I am tired. It's been a busy day, and I am not used to being out," she said. "Tomorrow will be better, my darling, as we go to my house."

Thorn closed her eyes and drifted off to sleep. As soon as I entered her presence again, I felt comforted and reassured. I was safe, and she would protect and help me. I relaxed and went to sleep with her arms wrapped around me. Maybe I was wrong. Maybe life with Thorn would be okay.

The next night, we stole a car and drove across London to her house, parking a few streets over and walking the last part to distance ourselves from the vehicle. I had been in too much of a daze and to star-struck in her presence to ask her anything meaningful since the prison break, but several questions had crossed my mind. On the walk to her house, I plucked up the courage to get some answers.

"What are we going to do next?" I asked.

Thorn looked around and grabbed my hand as we walked.

"We finish your training. I promised to make you a man," she answered.

"What does that mean?" I asked, unsure after the events in the prison cell.

"I need to train you to look after yourself. There are many skills you will need. Just the superior power isn't enough."

I didn't understand what these skills would be and just carried on walking. She must have sensed my uncertainty.

"No need to turn you into a vampire, as we have these ten needles and you are young. Best to spend eternity at a good physical age. Teenage vampires are very annoying, all that angst and hormones for eternity, urrg," she said, pulling a face and then laughing. "In the meantime, you can act as my daytime protector. You must learn to fight, and the ways of the underworld ready for your final everlasting change."

"Okay," I said, trying to take it all in.

"Many vampires, when changed, don't last the year, as they don't know the rules and how to control their powers. I can teach you all of this, and with each needle, you can practice and grow."

"Okay, so what about other vampires? Are we going to meet some soon?" I asked.

"In good time, be patient. First, we have unfinished business with Barry. He has seen something and recorded something of great danger to us. He must be dealt with."

The idea of going after Barry again filled me with fear and then satisfaction, as with Thorn and the needles I could beat him. I could exact my revenge.

We made it to the house. Thorn disappeared out into the back garden and came back with a key. For some reason, I expected a gothic mansion with wrought iron gates, an overgrown garden and bats flapping around in the air but this wasn't a film. The house was in a typical housing estate, an average detached three-bedroom house, single garage, a tidy front lawn and path. She opened up, and we walked inside.

"Not what you were expecting?"

"No," I answered, looking around the hallway.

"In the South of France, I have a gothic mansion with iron gates. We can visit it one day, but the garden is very tidy. Not sure if there are any bats," she said and sniggered.

I smiled and realised I needed to be more aware of my thoughts around a psychic vampire.

"You can live in the upstairs if you like. Three bedrooms upstairs to choose from," she said as we toured the rest of the house.

The house was clean and tidy and furnished in a modern fashion, very airy with bright colours on the walls. In the front room, leather sofas sat opposite a large TV. A small kitchen connected to the back garden. It looked like a showroom, but it was the house of a vampire.

"I have people who work for me that keep it clean. They make it looked lived in and pay the bills from the money I send on in case I ever disappear. It looks like the location of my house has remained safe. I can't sense any issues," Thorn said as she reopened her eyes.

"I only come up here at night. Like I said, you can live up here, or live with me in my apartment," she said and entered a number into a combination lock on the door under the stairs.

The door opened, and Thorn descended the bare wooden stairs into the basement. I followed. The lights came on to reveal a large room with an enormous king-sized bed in the middle of the oak flooring and a large TV screen on the wall opposite. A small kitchen area contained a fridge, microwave and a small hob.

"Shower room in the corner," she said, pointing over to the far corner of the room.

"In the other corner is my wardrobe," she said, pointing to the other corner next to a large mirror and an archway leading to racks of clothes.

"I doubt there is anything in there that would suit you. Unless you have another secret life you wish to tell me about," she said, smirking.

I looked at her, too bewildered to get the joke.

"Uh, no," I said.

I walked over to the huge bed with a big red velvety blanket over the top of it and a studded black leather headboard at the back. I ran my hand across the velvety blanket, feeling its soft fabric against my fingertips, wondering what future the room held for me. The walls and ceiling shone a passionate red illuminated from the spotlights in the ceiling. I stood by the bed looking around at the paintings of vampires, monsters and humans in different poses of loving and fighting. In one, it seemed to be both.

"I am fabulously rich. This is just one of many houses I own across the world. The upstairs is for night time and show, and the basement for daytime," she said.

Thorn switched on the TV and the local news sprung out.

"Police are still investigating the gang massacre in a London Park two nights ago and an attack on a group of men late last night. The police believe these incidents are connected. They wish to talk to a couple in connection with these crimes," a newsreader said.

A picture of me then flashed up on the screen.

"If you see this man, please contact the police. Please do not approach, he is considered extremely dangerous," the newsreader continued.

I turned to Thorn.

"They know I did it," I said.

"The other person is a woman," the newsreader said.

At that point, a photo fit of Thorn appeared on the screen.

"Again, please contact the police if you have any news. Do not approach either suspect. They are extremely dangerous."

She shrugged her shoulders. "They were drug dealers. I thought I got them all."

Now I knew where she went last night and where the money came from to buy clothes and food.

"I can't go back, can I?" I asked.

"Do you want to go back?"

"I don't know, I just didn't think it would be so final."

"You can leave at any time," she said, and pointed towards the stairs, "they may let you off. It's not the police you have to worry about, it's the 'Hunters'. They will want you back in the cells for samples and experiments."

"Oh," I said and sat on the edge of the bed.

More of my unanswered questions came to mind.

"How come you didn't leave me after you had escaped?" I asked.

Thorn looked over at me as she turned off the TV and put on some dance music.

"Why did you come back for me?" she asked instead.

"Because of what I had done. I had killed those guys in the park."

"Is that all of it? I was hoping for more," she replied, smiling and fluttering her eyelashes.

"You mean sex," I answered, and she nodded and smirked.

"Yes, I desired you, and you used your abilities to ensure that," I said, and she smiled, "but that was a trick. I had realised that very early on."

Thorn looked puzzled, walked over, sat next to me, and put her hand on my knee.

"Then why, if you knew it was a trick?"

"You looked so sad and lonely in that cell, and I knew just how you felt after the betrayal and violence I have suffered over the last year."

A small red tear appeared in the corner of her left eye, and she quickly wiped it away. She held my hand and looked into my eyes.

Her voice wavered for a second. "You see a lot. You are much more intelligent than I realised. You are still alive as you are right, what I desire more than anything in this world is a companion. I have been stuck in that cell for two years," she answered. "The others who come and work there have been taught to ignore me, and they ensure they are never left alone long enough with me to be influenced. I heard their thoughts while in that cell. I knew what they were trying to make and that those two needles had the power to transform someone temporarily into a vampire. When you came in, I realised we could help each other. I could help you have your revenge, and I believed you would return once you had taken the formula. I felt your anger and pain and showed you those needles so you could get revenge. I just hoped my hypnotic powers would be enough to get you to return."

I absorbed it all in. "So what's next?"

"What do you want?"

"I don't want to be scared anymore, not to be bullied or beaten up, to be someone other people fear."

Thorn nodded. "I still want a companion. I don't want to be alone anymore. I want to share it with someone."

"So we have a deal?" I asked, "You teach me never to be scared again, and I will never leave you."

"Yes, a deal," and we shook hands, "I can't stop you being scared again, but I can teach you to control it and use it. Even vampires get scared," she said as we shook.

I felt disappointed; it must have shown as I stopped shaking hands and pulled away. Thorn pulled me back and stared into my eyes.

"You must learn to embrace your emotions and use them to fuel you. Bathe in your fear, your lust, your love and it will make you stronger. Denying your emotions, good or bad, is a waste of good energy. There is so much to be gained through fear."

"Okay," I said, kind of understanding and nodded my head.

"It won't be easy though. It will be tough," she added.

"Yeah, it is okay. I understand."

"Good, let's seal the deal," she said, lying down on the bed, pulling me on top of her and kissing me.

We made love again but without the swirling mists and her other powers seducing me. I didn't mind, as her body and passion were more than enough for anyone. Afterwards, as I laid in the bed recovering, Thorn got up and walked into her wardrobe. She pulled on a pair of tracksuit bottoms and a vest top. She threw over a pair of shorts.

"Try these on and put your t-shirt back on. The night is young. We might as well start on your training," she said.

I dressed as eager to get started, and Thorn stood in the space between the bed and wardrobe.

"We should have enough space here," she said, and I stood opposite her.

"Ready," I said and nodded.

"Okay, hit me."

I threw a feeble punch at her, worried about hurting her for some reason. She looked at me with disdain as she moved out of the way.

"Hit me," she said.

I tried again but not much better than before.

"Use your emotions, pretend I am someone you hate," she said.

I imagined Barry.

"Close your eyes and picture them. Let those emotions of hate and anger build up 'til you are ready to burst."

I relived the mugging and the picture of him with Scarlett. The anger swelled up, and it pumped around my body as it had done before when I tried to take the needles.

I flashed back into the moment again, lying on the floor as Barry kicked me in the stomach and encouraged his friends to join in. The pain of the kicks thumping into my back and legs, my arms shielding my face, abusive taunts filling the air and spit running down my cheeks, and Barry filming it all and laughing. The final threat punctuated with a fist hitting my nose, and then my head slamming into the pavement. I had revenge on all of them except Barry. He escaped, and I still wanted him dead. The anger of his survival intensified my rage 'til it reached new heights.

"When you are ready, open your eyes and let it take you."

My eyes opened, and I launched a fist at her. She parried and moved away quickly.

"Good, remember what you are fighting for. Now keep that feeling and control it."

I didn't wait for any more instructions, launching a flurry of fists and random kicks in her direction. I had let my emotions fill me with energy.

"Good. Now control it. Use it with intent. Focus on your goal and your aim."

I focused on punching her in the head, fist after fist, legs pumping me forward, trying to get through to her and make a connection. Thorn skipped out the way, circled around me and clipped me on the ear as she moved.

"More," she shouted.

I charged at her repeatedly until she stepped to the side and flung me, face first, onto the bed.

"Good, you have discovered your aggression and desire to fight. You will need them where I am going to take you."

I pushed back off the bed and charged at her headfirst, trying to tackle her as she talked. But she spun out of the way at the last moment, sending me headfirst into her wardrobe. I laid on the floor, face in her shoes, and her skirts and dresses had fallen on top of me.

Thorn laughed.

"Nice try, good instincts," she said and helped me back to my feet, "let me show you some moves."

She showed me how to stand correctly, and we went through various punches and kicks. I practised trying to hit her and then defended against her measured attacks. We carried on for a couple of hours of training, and then stopped and showered off.

Thorn waited in bed for me as I dried off.

"Tomorrow, we go out shopping. We both need more clothes. Also, I will need some more blood from you tomorrow to keep me going. Is that okay?"

"Yes, of course," I answered. She would have to feed, and it made the bond between us stronger. After all, I had some of her blood in terms of the needles.

"I can't keep drinking from you. It's just until we are settled. You will need all your strength for the training," she said.

"It's okay. I understand you need to feed."

"Let us sleep now. We are both tired and tomorrow will be a full night," she said, pulling back the covers for me to join her.

I bounded in, and she wrapped her arms around me and went to sleep. My heart filled with joy at being enveloped in her arms again. I had started my journey to becoming a man and then a vampire.

CHAPTER FOURTEEN

It was a Friday afternoon, and it had been two weeks since I had killed the gang in the park and rescued Thorn from her prison cell. In that time, Thorn kept to her side of the deal and trained me every night. I expected to learn fighting skills, and I did, but it also went far beyond combat training and into skills on how to survive and hide. I learnt about creating new identities, as I couldn't carry on as Jonathan Harper after the incidents two weeks ago.

Plus, I learnt computer hacking to infiltrate our enemies and create my new identities. I was learning to drive a car and ride a motorbike, so I could get about quickly and get us shelter before sunlight. I started studying Spanish, as it was one of the most popularly spoken languages in the world. There would be more to come, but she had congratulated me on my quick progression. Top of the class in vampire school, with Thorn setting me homework to do while she slept.

I completed my boxing practice, revised my Spanish homework for the day, and then went shopping at the local supermarket. I put the food away, and as I did, I dragged out the back of the freezer a packet of fish fingers. Stuffed inside the packet was a plastic bag, and wrapped inside the bag were money and a map. The money and map were part of my escape plan.

During the daylight hours, I stayed uncertain about my time with Thorn and longed for a normal life, which I knew was impossible. Those thoughts I had on my first night alone came flooding back every day while she slept because I could think freely and explore my true emotions. Free not to have to fill my mind with junk to protect myself. Free to think about what I genuinely wanted.

I pulled out the money and counted it, one hundred pounds, and I added another ten pounds left over from the shopping. I reviewed the map and visually traced the route from Thorn's house to the research centre. I pretended to drive the route using Google Street View, and I had memorised the route, so I didn't need the map, just in case. I would use the money to buy things for the escape, a phone to call ahead, and UV light to defend myself in case she tried to hunt me down.

In the meantime, I wanted to learn more, and maybe another injection or two wouldn't be a bad thing either. I could go back home as a proper man, bigger, stronger and more experienced in life. I could be a real boyfriend and win Scarlett back. I couldn't go anywhere until I finished what I had started with Barry. I didn't want him coming back after me, looking for his own revenge.

That night, my nerves returned as I waited for Thorn to rise, wondering if this would be the night she killed me. However, as soon as she woke up, I felt comfort and reassurance in her company. It was a feeding night. I would need to be on alert for potential problems. Thorn needed to feed every other day to keep going. I guessed we would head off to the usual spots, hoping to catch some prey.

Thorn woke up hungry and satiated her bloody thirst with a rare steak. She could eat, and it helped, but it was no replacement for blood. She liked to eat and drink, as it helped to keep her identity as a normal human when out at night. Her metabolism worked fast and caused the high heat she generated. It meant that the alcohol burnt through her quickly. She would get drunk fast but sober up just as quickly. She preferred to take her alcohol in the bloodstream of her victims. The intoxication lasted longer and came on slower, allowing her to control herself.

Thorn dressed in something sexy but comfortable, as quick reactions would be needed. Trousers and sturdy boots were the order of the night.

There were a few rough areas nearby that Thorn usually frequented when looking to feed, and we headed to one of those first. The time approached nine o'clock at night, and we entered the area looking for a place to park. I would stay with the car while Thorn walked around by herself, flashing her Gucci handbag, pretending to be helpless, rich and stupid. I would stay with the car to protect it and remain in radio contact with Thorn the whole time. We both had earpieces connected, and Thorn carried a GPS locator, which I followed on my smartphone. If Thorn needed a quick escape, I could drive around to pick her up, and we would be away before anyone knew. Likewise, if I ran into trouble, Thorn could be back in a flash. Her training and techniques extended far beyond what I expected in a vampire, and she used whatever technology she could find to give herself an edge.

On other nights out, I was always surprised how many good Samaritans tried to direct her off the streets and into safety. They were worried she would be attacked and robbed. Thorn always thanked them and moved on down the street out of their sight. I was equally surprised at which people would help and which would attack. Over the weeks, I learnt to spot the good ones from the bad ones. Thorn always knew, but she had her vampire senses to alert her. Eventually, someone would see her as an opportunity and make a fatal mistake. Thorn would get her feed.

That night we didn't even get to park the car, as a police car pulled us over as we drove along the main street. The young policeman warned us to turn around and go home, as it wasn't safe. When asked why, he mentioned several recent bloody attacks that had left their victims dead or hurt, as having lost a lot of blood. When Thorn fed, she would cover up the fang marks with a cut and would try not to take from the neck, as it would draw the attention of the Hunters. The policeman never suspected her as the culprit behind the recent attacks. No one ever did.

We headed into a nightclub instead, and I watched with drinks in hand as she pushed her way into the middle of the dance floor, and started dancing as if she lived in a seductive world of her own. Her raven tousled hair swaying about, and her body dancing to the rhythm beating out of the speakers. The lights flashed in coordination with the trashy euro dance music belting out.

It didn't take long before she got the attention of a group of men who tried to dance along with her, each of them trying to take the lead over the others. She danced between all three, shaking her body and making sure they got an eyeful of what they needed.

The loud music and amount of people in the place made it nearly impossible for Thorn to read minds, as the noise was just too loud and too many voices to focus on. She told me she could pick up the odd thought of those close to her. With the thoughts of just the three men, she was deciding which one would make the best meal. I still had the earpiece in and could hear the odd shouted comment to her.

Eventually, she picked one, grabbed him by the hand and dragged him off the dance floor. They stood at the side, shared his drink for a few minutes, and then kissed. Next, Thorn led him off to a private spot, usually the toilets or an alleyway out the back.

She made sure I saw them kissing and groping, and smiled over at me as she finished, purposefully trying to make me jealous. I listened to the whole thing in my earpiece as they carried on in the toilets until Thorn decided to feed. A sudden thump, followed by the sounds of cutting and gulping of blood. I walked out of the nightclub and waited outside, knowing she wouldn't be far behind. Thorn appeared after a few minutes, grinning as her thirst quenched and intoxicated from the alcohol in her victim.

"I need another before we go home," she said, and we drove off to another nightclub a few miles away to distance ourselves.

"Is he dead?" I asked on the way.

"No. I only took about a pint. He will be weak for a day or so but will recover. That's why I need another one tonight."

Thorn had her own twisted moral code when it came to feeding. If they attacked her, it was fair game to kill them and drain them dry, or at least get her fill, which inevitably left them near dead. If she had entrapped someone, like in the nightclub, she would only take what she needed and leave them to live another day.

"Do you have to kiss them and go so far with them before feeding?" I asked, jealous of having to endure another man with her again.

"Oh Jon, they deserve something to make it worth their while." She laughed and pressed her foot against the accelerator forcing the car to surge towards the next nightclub.

This formed another part of her hunting code, give them something to remember her by, so they would struggle to understand what had happened, but she insisted she didn't have sex with them. She pushed thoughts into their minds, telling them they had slipped over and cut themselves.

"Didn't your Mum tell you not to play with your food?" I said and crossed my arms, but she laughed again.

"That's hilarious. I think you are jealous. You have to remember I have been around a few more years than you."

"I know, but I can't help it."

"Don't worry, Jon. I am keeping to our deal. You are my companion. He was just sustenance."

At the next nightclub, she went through the same routine, but this time, she took her victim to the alley out the back for a quick exit. I watched as three girls followed her down the stairs and into the back alley. I let her know.

"You have three women on your trail," I said, knowing her earpiece would receive the message.

"I used to be a singer in a band called the Leeches," Thorn said to her victim.

"Really," he replied.

This was one of our codes so that I knew she had received the message. Good, she would be prepared. She would have probably detected them anyway and unlikely to be in any trouble, but it allowed me to play my part as her protector.

The gang of girls walked as quick as their tight skirts would let them down the dark alleyway, with their high heels splashing through the shallow puddles on the ground. One of them grabbed a bit of broken wood from the side of the alley and held it like a club as they moved in. I waited for Thorn to signal me for help but she didn't. Thorn and her victim

The Birth of Vengeance

stopped kissing as they detected the girls approaching.

"That's my boyfriend, you leave him alone," a blonde girl yelled. Her hair had been scraped back into a ponytail and face plastered in makeup. Her fat pushed against the seams of a tight red dress. She looked horrible and scary in a different way than I was used to.

"He is a grown boy. I am sure he can make his own choices," Thorn replied, with no sign of emotion.

"I wasn't doing anything. Michelle, I promise," the man pleaded.

Thorn let go of his arm, and he walked over to Michelle. She slapped him backhanded across his face. Her gold sovereign rings cut his mouth, leaving his face red and body shaking.

"Get out of here, you prick and go home," she screamed into his face.

He recoiled, holding his bruised jaw, and he looked at Thorn.

"Sorry," he said and received another smack on the back of his head as he walked away, making him stumble forward. He walked back to the nightclub and saw me laughing to myself.

Behind him, the girls had surrounded Thorn.

"Going to teach you a lesson, little Miss Perfect. After I am finished with you, no bloke will want you," Michelle said, sneering and her friend slapped the broken wood into her own hand.

I looked forward to watching, but the scolded boyfriend approached, and he scowled at me.

"What you laughing at?" he said.

"Nothing."

"Bullshit," he said, red faced from the slap and wanting to regain some pride.

He pushed me back into the wall. I pushed myself off it and shoved back, making him stagger backwards. He charged in and swung a fist. My instincts took over. I ducked, and rugby-tackled him to the floor and then rolled back onto my feet. I was scared and reacted from instinct. I tried to let my anger pour through me by thinking about the mugging, but I didn't have time.

He returned to his feet and punched at me again. I put my hands over my head, absorbed a couple of blows and then fired one back into his face, making him step away. I followed up with a couple more, which he dodged, and then he caught me square on the chin with a punch. I dropped to the floor. He stood over me, ready to follow up, when Thorn appeared in front of him and launched him off his feet into the alleyway wall.

Back down the alley, the three girls were rolling on the floor in pain, covering their clothes in grime and rain. Thorn cut open the man's arm and crouched over him like a predator feeding on their kill. Yet another typical night when hunting with Thorn, as I often got embroiled in the fights. I got the impression it was part of my training.

CHAPTER FIFTEEN

Six weeks had passed since joining forces with Thorn, and my day and night lives were becoming acutely distinct. The days filled with plans of what could happen if I left and the new life I could lead. Maybe Scarlett and I could forgive each other. I could work for the government and let them test me in return for safety.

During the day, I revisited those old daydreams of living with Scarlett and the normal things we would do as a couple. I wished I could be back on that sofa, snuggled up watching a film together. In the meantime, I collected more money and stored it in the bag in the freezer. I practised the route home and investigated getting a UV lamp. During the rest of the day, I continued with my training, building my skills and muscles.

The night was all about time with Thorn: training, fighting, feeding, dancing and passion. I would be scared as the night came, and then sad to see it go as I enjoyed being with Thorn and the excitement it brought.

In the daytime, I would be happy to be myself, with my own thoughts and desires, not having to fill my mind so Thorn couldn't read my feelings. However, recently I had to do this less and less, as at night thoughts of escape and Scarlett never returned. At night, I only thought about Thorn and revenge on Barry. I had become two different people, Day Jonathan and Night Jonathan.

Day Jonathan wanted it to all end and find a way back home to Scarlett. Night Jonathan wanted it never to end. Night enjoyed the violence, sex and training, and looked forward to the final revenge on Barry, and then expanding out into the rest of the vampire world.

That day had special significance, as it was the day of the kidnapping trial in Leeds against the three O'Keefe brothers. I should have been there giving evidence against them, and if convicted, it would probably stop Giles' Mum's case for dangerous driving. I hoped they would still get a conviction, even though my evidence was critical having been the only eyewitness to all the events on that day, and the events of the previous ten years of bullying as well. The killing of the gang and rescuing Thorn had meant I couldn't attend. I would check the Internet later for any news.

Night descended, and I became Night Jonathan, looking forward to our activities. Thorn and I sat in the car outside a nightclub in the area I went to college, watching and waiting for Barry, as we knew he frequented it. The alternative nightclub played pretty much anything except pop music, and the clientele comprised a raw cross-section of people and music types from the surrounding areas. The nightclub was called, "Excite"; and the sign's green fluorescent letters curled and glowed out in the dark above two worn blue doors with the paint peeling off.

I sat in the passenger's seat of Thorn's black BMW, with tinted windows, leather seats, aircon and all the top of the range trimmings. The car sat across the other side of the road, in the shadows about twenty meters away. Other vehicles had parked all around us on this side of the street, and the other side remained empty.

We had watched the door for over an hour and I was getting bored. I wanted to go inside and search for him, but Thorn advised not to, as Hunters would be looking for us. I asked Thorn about the Hunters a few days after her escape and their attempt to stop us. Thorn explained they had captured her, and they were an organisation hunting down and killing vampires normally, but things had changed recently as they now seemed involved with the government and research. If we were looking for Barry, they were probably watching him in the hope we would return.

I shifted in my seat and felt the cold metal of my gun in my hand, a Browning nine millimetre High Powered Semi-Automatic Pistol. Thorn's training had recently gone beyond hand-to-hand. Thorn had been training me in Thai boxing, as it resembled the vampire martial art style of fighting. Thai boxing is known as the science of the eight limbs, and the vampire style is similar by adding in the razor sharp claws and fangs of a vampire. It is a direct style of fighting to take the opposition down, nothing fancy just a clean, direct kill.

We moved on to fighting with small blades, to mimic the claws of a vampire so I would be prepared for whenever I made the changes through the needles. The plan eventually would progress onto swords, and she had a couple of Japanese Katana swords for us to practice with once I had mastered the small blades.

Only yesterday we moved on to guns. Thorn didn't like guns as vampires fought better close up using their superior speed and strength. In a gunfight, the battlefield levelled out between humans and vampires, but I wasn't a vampire yet, and a gun would allow me to protect us.

In the basement of her house, behind the picture of the werewolf and vampire fighting, was a concealed weapons rack. A button under the bed slid the wall back, revealing a rack of swords, knives, throwing stars, machine guns and pistols.

From this rack, she had chosen the Browning pistol for me and loaded it up, and then we drove to a deserted warehouse to practice shooting tin cans on an upturned box. It felt like an old western shooting tin cans but it did the trick. I learnt quickly with Thorn's guidance, and her psychic abilities pushing in the right images and feelings into my head. The Hunters had machine guns and knives, and I needed to know how to fire back to defend myself and protect Thorn, especially during the daylight hours.

The music played from the car stereo, breaking up the monotony of waiting and watching. Thorn shifted in her seat, and her tight denim jeans rubbed against the leather seats. She stretched her feet in her red leather knee-high boots and adjusted her short black leather jacket with red stripes down the arms. Underneath the jacket, she wore a black vest.

I got bored and restless in the car, while Thorn stayed patient and focused her senses at the nightclub and her surroundings. I guessed that patience came with age. Yet, I didn't know how old Thorn was, but on a couple of occasions, she mentioned events from history and I had tried to work it out. She had mentioned the hundred year war, which made her at least seven hundred years old, but I think she went back even further. She continued to be tight-lipped about her history.

I tried to break the silence and relax us both for a second.

"Thorn, what do you call an asthmatic vampire?" I asked.

"I don't know," she said.

"Vlad the Inhaler," I answered, giving a slight laugh to show it was a joke.

Thorn looked over and frowned.

"No more jokes," she said.

We went back to sitting in silence, waiting for something to happen.

People came and went from the nightclub but no one I recognised. People pushed open the two blue doors and stumbled out into the dark night. The fluorescent sign offered some light around the entrance and tainted those coming and going in its glow. Groups of people walked into the nightclub dressed up in gothic clothes and a few girls in nightclub small skirts and tops.

Two girls walked out of the blue nightclub doors, and the music followed them breaking into the quiet night outside. They both had dark hair, one short bobbed, and the other long and wavy, and they were both dressed in a rock chick style. The short-haired girl wore jeans, black boots and white t-shirt showing under her red leather jacket. She wore heavy black eyeliner and had a pirate skull nose stud, and each ear was pierced with three crucifixes. It took a moment to break out the features from the clothes she wore, but it was unmistakably Mary. She obviously found a new friend, as that couldn't be Scarlett with that hair colour.

The woman with the long dark wavy hair stumbled slightly as she lost control of her feet encased in heavy purple platform boots. Her hair swept around, concealing her face, and her friend grabbed her by her black leather jacket and pulled her up straight. They both giggled and staggered off. Above her boots, fishnet stockings led to a denim skirt and on her top, under the jacket, she wore a low-cut red shirt. She swished her hair back, showing black patches of makeup around her eyes and full black lips. Her ears decorated with ascending gold hoops and a gold chain around her pale neck. She looked familiar.

They giggled as they staggered down the street when a rough looking man wearing dirty denim burst out the doors. He was tall and sported a grubby goatee. He staggered about a bit, looking up and down the streets when he saw the two girls walking off.

"Scarlett, come back!"

She turned around, and her long wavy hair swished in the half-light of the cold winter's air. I recognised the way the hair moved. It was Scarlett. However, this wasn't my Scarlett as I remembered her. She had changed beyond recognition into something else or someone else. I didn't even think about what to do next. As soon as I recognised her, I clambered out of the car, slammed the door and walked over.

"Have another drink, come on, you owe me," the rough guy shouted.

"Get lost," Scarlett yelled and turned around to walk off when she saw me marching across the road to her.

I had dressed for comfort that night in jeans, a black hooded top and trainers. My hair had been trimmed right back into a stylish short cut with spikes gelled up. She took a moment to recognise me, same for her I guessed, out of context situation and a different look. But my determined march over had made her pay attention.

"Jon," she said, arms flung out.

I ran the last steps into her arms and hugged her tight. I didn't know why I did this after everything that had happened. Maybe instinct took over, as I was happy to see her after all that I had been through. Perhaps due to her intoxication, she appeared pleased to see me as well. As I hugged her, I heard fast footsteps approaching from behind, and I realised what an enormous mistake I had just made. I let go and stood back to take in her new look.

"You've changed," I said, admiring the black makeup, piercings and newly dyed hair.

Scarlett looked at me; her eyebrows raised.

"Look who's talking," she responded, eyeing me up and down, then looking at my side as Thorn's hand grabbed my hand and squashed it under her firm grasp. I grimaced, trying not to let the pain show.

I dreaded what might happen next, and I looked around at Thorn and offered an apologetic smile. Her face cool and calm, but I could sense seething anger beneath the surface.

"What happened to you?" Scarlett asked, looking at Thorn.

"You know stuff happens, you have to deal with it," I answered.

"It's all true then, what the news has been saying about you and her," Scarlett said, looking at Thorn.

I realised her comments referred to the news of the gang murders, the drug dealers Thorn killed on her first night and a few other minor incidents. I didn't know how to answer the question, and I didn't have to, as the drunk rough looking guy had continued stumbling towards us. He grabbed Scarlett's arm.

"She is with me kid, now get lost," he said and wrenched her arm.

Before I had time to react, Thorn stepped across and kicked him in the groin. There was nothing like a man attacking a woman to incense Thorn, and she was already boiling with anger. He dropped to the floor and onto one knee, and looked back up as Thorn followed up with a right hook bang on his jaw. His head snapped around fast, and he skidded down the pavement from the force of the blow, leaving a trail of blood coming from his face as it acted as a brake on the rough ground.

Thorn turned around to glare at Scarlett and me, and then she looked straight past us into the dark.

"Hunters," she shouted and shoved us all to the ground as shots rang over our heads.

"Go into the club and find a way out the back. I will meet you there," Thorn shouted as the shots continued.

I pulled out my gun and fired into the dark, and it seemed to be enough to allow Thorn to run for cover behind the row of cars. I grabbed Scarlett and Mary and pushed them back towards the front door as bullets smashed into the brickwork, spattering us with dust. I fired again and again in the vain hope it helped, as two men in black suits ran towards us with pistols firing. Scarlett and Mary bundled through the front door and crashed to the floor. I followed on not far behind when pain ripped through my lower leg. I lost my balance and crashed through the door, and then into Scarlett and Mary, creating a heap on the floor. A bullet had dissected the flesh of my right calf muscle.

The bouncers approached, and I turned the gun on them.

"Back off. I just want the exit," I shouted, and they raised their hands and moved backwards.

Scarlett and Mary pulled me to my feet, and I hobbled into the club. All the time, I kept the gun pointed at the bouncers and forced them to stay in the entrance hall.

Inside the nightclub, the circular dance floor in the middle overflowed with people jumping and head banging to some thrash metal band. We pushed past the other revellers around the sides of the dance floor and those queuing at the bar shouting for drinks. A few people looked around, then saw the gun in my hand and backed off in a panic. The music banged, and the red, blue and green lights flashed into my eyes, and the intense pain overwhelmed me.

I pushed through the pain, using my anger and fear to drive myself forward, just as Thorn had taught me. Mary knew the club well and directed us through the throng of people to the fire exit, and then out onto a small fire stairwell used by the revellers for smoking. I coughed on the cigarette smoke as we walked out onto the stairwell. The people outside panicked and hurried out of the way upon seeing the gun and the blood on my leg.

The top of the stairs had a small landing area connected to the back door of the nightclub, and the stairs went down one flight into a small car park at the back where the staff parked. A gate on the back of the car park stopped non-paying guests from sneaking in the back way.

I felt cold. The smell of cigarettes still permutated the air.

"You two need a moment. I will keep an eye out," Mary said and walked back inside.

I leant against the wall, taking the weight off my shot leg as the blood poured out. I hoped Thorn wouldn't take too long. I should have probably got some first aid training as well.

"What the hell is going on with you?" Scarlett asked, looking at my gun in disbelief.

"I can't explain. It isn't safe to know," I answered, trying to focus through the pain.

"People came to question me after the incident in the park. They told me to tell you, if I ever saw you again, it's not too late. They will understand. They will look after you. You can have your life back. It's the woman they want and a formula," Scarlett said.

Her statement surprised me, as she seemed to know everything.

"So you know what happened in the park?"

"No, I just know those boys are dead, and those people asking questions suggested you were involved. I didn't understand the rest about a formula and a woman. I guess that was her earlier."

"That will be those people who just shot me."

"You shot at them as well. Give it a chance. We could be together again. There is a way out," she said.

I looked at her, and I wanted to believe it could be true, but the images of her with Barry were emblazoned into my memory.

"It's a bit late for that. Remember?"

"I can explain everything, just come back, trust me."

The thoughts I had in the daytime came flooding back. Maybe it wasn't just a fantasy. I could go back. Scarlett still wanted me. I could forgive her if she could forgive me and accept what I had become and what I had done. I could have a life with her after all, get a flat, go to university and do normal things together.

"I am working on it," I said, smiling briefly, allowing myself to be Day Jonathan and thought about the plan I was hatching during the daytime. Then I sensed something, a feeling of being watched.

A massive bang sounded on the stairs, and the metal vibrated under our feet. Thorn had dropped from the rooftop onto the fire exit stairs, and I returned to Night Jonathan again.

"He is mine," Thorn shouted, eyes glowing red at Scarlett.

Scarlett backed off from the sudden entrance and threat. Thorn's red eyes had done the trick, and Scarlett's face pulled back in panic, exposing the sobering whites of her eyes. She backed into the railings on the stairs and looked about for an urgent exit. Scarlett put her hands out in front of her in a feeble attempt to block, as Thorn closed in with eyes still burning red.

"You're after Barry, aren't you?" Scarlett asked.

"Yes," she answered.

"He is at his cousin's house, Terry."

I nodded. "Thank you."

"Are you going to kill him?"

I didn't hesitate with my answer. "Yes."

"Good," Scarlett said, her voice spitting venom, and the strength of her feelings surprised me. I always thought I would come back to find them as a couple, as if none of it mattered.

The sounds of sirens pierced the night. Thorn looked around at me and spotted the blood pouring from my leg.

"Those sirens are for us. I need to get you home," Thorn said.

"Before you go, I heard some news from friends in Leeds," Scarlett said.

"What?"

"The kidnapping trial of your friend never made it to court. Without you, the case wasn't strong enough, so they decided not to proceed. Instead, they went ahead with the other case, and your friend's Mum has been found guilty of dangerous driving and received six months in prison."

"Those bastards," I said.

They had gotten away with the kidnapping due to my disappearance. Yet more anguish to add to the guilt I already felt for leaving Giles with them on that day and then ignoring him when back in school, which led to his suicide attempt. I had the chance to make it all okay, and I had made a mess of it because of Barry and his gang, and my own selfish desires. Giles' Mum, Linda, had been punished for trying to protect her son. Life wasn't fair.

Thorn looked at me puzzled, as I hadn't told her about my past in Leeds.

"You can tell me about this later. We have to leave now," Thorn said.

She scooped me onto her shoulders and jumped over the railings into the car park below. She raced off and hurdled over the six foot high gate. Scarlett leant against the barrier as two bouncers came bursting through. Her jaw agape at Thorn's supernatural power, and she waved as I disappeared into the night.

CHAPTER SIXTEEN

She flung me into the back seat, jumped into the front and then wheel spun away.

"You will be okay," Thorn shouted from the front seat.

"huh," I said.

"Talk to me, don't go to sleep."

But in the safety of the warm car, my mind relaxed, and the welcome fog of unconsciousness waved over me. I drifted into a dream of being back in school in Leeds with my best friend, Giles.

A cold shock jolted my body awake. I wiped the cold water off my face and winced from the lights in the room as my eyes adjusted. I regained focus, sensing a blurry figure pacing up and down in front of me. The steps thumped on the hard floor, and the head and eyes focused on me the whole time. As my eyes adjusted to the light, Thorn's face in full vampire flow, with eyes red and fangs sticking out, came into view. Her fury painted in her vampire features and her body glowed an angry red. I leant back and felt the base of the bed behind me and realised I was back in Thorn's basement.

"You idiot," she shouted, jumping inches from my face, fangs cutting the air.

"Sorry, sorry. I ... I ... I didn't think. I just reacted. I just followed my emotions like you said," I answered.

"Don't you dare try to turn this on to me. You are a werewolf's hair away from being ripped apart."

"I'm sorry, I just got carried away."

The wound in my leg remained untreated, and blood had pooled around it. I was in big trouble. I needed help soon before I bled out.

Thorn glanced down at the pool of blood with its red sticky sight and smell that was enticing her to feed. The thirst and rage created a lethal combination. I knew from first-hand experience from my own time as a vampire in the park. It was as if I had covered myself in raw meat, jumped into the lion's den and shouted to get its attention. I just hoped for mercy, no matter how small, in order to survive.

"I am sorry I have upset you. I just wanted to say hello," I said, knowing I had to distract her from the meal pouring from my leg.

"Say hello! You nearly got us both killed. Scarlett and your friends betrayed you, remember? I have only ever looked after you, and this is how you repay me," she shouted, fangs snapping only inches from my face. Her fangs dripped with saliva as the hunger manifested into physical form.

"I am sorry. You are right. We have a deal," I answered.

"A deal, is that it?" she snapped back. She rocked back on her feet and placed a hand behind to regain her balance. Her bottom lip wobbled and eyes welled up with misty red tears.

"No," I said.

I paused, as I was misjudging this situation. She wasn't just angry. She was also jealous and upset. Jealous of my relationship with Scarlett and the fact my feelings for her hadn't gone. Upset I didn't think more of our relationship beyond the deal. But at night, I did think of it as more than just a deal. I just never thought she did.

I took a gamble to fix the situation, as I was getting myself into more and more trouble. She would break any second. I had to do something.

"You are right. It was unforgivable. I haven't learnt to forget my past yet, but I will learn with your help." I said.

She stared a little more restrained, and the misty red tears in her eyes retreated. I followed up and pulled my hooded jumper to one side, revealing my neck and turning it towards her.

"You are hungry. You need to eat, take whatever you want. I belong to you," I said, supplementing the offer of my neck.

I was bluffing, hoping it would show her my loyalty, and if I were wrong, it would be just a bit of blood.

Only a slight pause passed before the fangs pierced through my skin and the blood flowed out of my body. I accepted the sacrifice I needed to make to keep alive and wrapped my arms around her and pulled her close.

Her body grew even warmer than usual in the throes of feeding on me, so I took some comfort in the heat as she drank my blood. She wrapped her arms around my body, squeezing me tight and pumping hard. Her legs straddled me as she forced the blood out into her mouth. She was really going for it.

The pressure of her arms crushed my ribs and squeezed the blood out of my chest. I gasped for breath as my lungs and airways buckled under the pressure. My bones cracked, sending pulses of excruciating pain through my body. I screamed, a breathless scream, on each crack of my ribs, and it resonated through my body until it sounded inside my skull.

She squeezed her thighs around my waist, crushing my stomach and pumping the blood into her mouth. I had already lost a lot of blood through the gunshot wound, but Thorn sucked harder and deeper, filling her body and satisfying her thirst.

I went weak all over, arms and legs unable to move, but she wasn't going to stop. I summoned my remaining strength and tried to push her away, but to no effect. I tried one last time fighting as hard as I could, arms and legs thrashing in a final death throw, hitting her on the back and head, trying to get her to stop. She didn't even register the blows, but just squeezed even harder and harder, sucking deeper and deeper until it all went black, and I couldn't feel anything.

I drifted off to a strange sleep with images of Thorn and Scarlett flashing before my mind. I flashed back to events over the last year; the car accident, Giles crying, kissing Scarlett and sleeping with Thorn.

A bright light pierced through the submerging darkness with a hand reaching out, accompanied by a woman calling my name. I didn't recognise the voice, but it felt comforting. I reached out to the hand of light, and my fingertips touched it, and a warm, happy sensation ran from my finger ends into the rest of my body. A woman's face emerged from the light, her mouth and eyes coming into focus. I knew this person. A sharp stab hit my arm. The face retreated, and the hand of light sucked back into a black hole, circling into the darkness.

A burning heat spread across my body from the stabbing. My nerve endings twitched as it networked its way across my system. My muscles contorted from the scorching heat, and it spread through to my extremities. I snapped back wide-awake and alive, panting for breath like someone who had come up for air from being trapped deep underwater. Thorn watched from a crouched position a meter away, and her frown turned to a small smile.

"You are back," she said, breathing out heavily and placing her hands on top of her head.

An empty needle laid on the floor a couple of meters away, and the puncture mark on my forearm disappeared. The wound on my leg was healing, flesh knitting back together, covering up the bare muscles underneath. I roared in agony as my ribs snapped back into place, healing and reshaping. My stomach followed suit, as the collapsed muscles healed and pushed back into their regular position. As I roared, my eyes turned red, fangs broke out, and claws ripped through the ends of my fingers. I touched my neck to find the bite marks had gone. The vampire formula had saved my life.

I sprung off the floor towards Thorn's neck with my claws released. I caught her by surprise, crashing into her, knocking her over, and rolling on top of her, face to snarling face. She kicked me off and sprung to her feet. I jumped back up and charged again. She moved with lightning speed and pinned me to the wall by my throat.

"Cool it," she growled.

I snarled back, fangs bared and snapping. She squeezed my throat to prove her strength. I stared into her red eyes, and my vampire reflection bounced back. My fangs ripped at the air, and my eyes blazed the same as hers. I focused, bringing it under control, knowing this wasn't a fight I could win. Thorn had hundreds of years' experience, and I had a brief few hours. My eyes returned to normal and fangs retracted. Thorn lowered me to the floor and retreated to the edge of the bed and sat facing me. I breathed in deep, hands on my knees, trying hard to bring my power under control.

"I am sorry. You are new to all this. Maybe I should be more understanding," she said, relaxing her body and looking down at the floor, her voice high pitched and apologetic.

I glared at her, not sure what to say.

She continued. "I accept you were sorry. You are brave offering yourself to me like that in my state. Don't ever do it again. There may be no way back next time."

I nodded in agreement. It was an easy request to accept.

She looked up at me again. "Most vampires choose a new name after they have turned. It helps to distance themselves from their past and begin their new life. This may help if you choose a new vampire name," Thorn said, still speaking in an apologetic tone, trying to appease me.

"I will think about it," I said, not taking too much notice of the idea.

We sat in silence for a moment, and I tried to gather my thoughts and senses under the influence of the vampire formula. I stood upright and leant against the wall, looking straight at Thorn, trying to work out my next move. She looked down at the floor, hands in her lap, palms facing up, legs crossed with one of them jigging up and down. I had never seen her so submissive; when in the prison cell, she was sad but not upset. I guessed this counted as our first argument, and I hoped they wouldn't always be this deadly.

"We should make use of your change. I can teach you how to control your vampire powers, and you can practice," Thorn said, breaking the painful silence with her voice more in control again and regaining her natural authority.

I nodded in agreement, as it seemed like a good way to move on. I wanted her back to her usual self. It scared me to see her so downbeat and feelings of forgiveness for her attack had emerged. Anyway, I had an excess of energy that needed burning off before I could think straight again. I went and sat beside her on the bed, and she turned around to face me. Her body posture was more confident, and her legs remained still, as she resumed her natural state as my mentor and lover.

Thorn showed me how to change my vampire features and how to use the rest of my senses to best effect. We sparred for a bit as now on equal terms, vampire against vampire, blazing around the house, taking it in turns to attack and defend. We would stop in between attacks, and Thorn praised my good combinations and improved my weaker moves. She taught me the limit of my powers and how best to use them in a fight as a vampire.

I'd entered a whole new game, vampire against vampire, and I realised how much more I needed to learn. However, I was improving. On one occasion I knocked Thorn to the floor, but not for long as she sprang back up and front kicked me through the door in the upstairs bedroom, and I crashed down the stairs. Thorn remained the better fighter, but my progress had impressed her.

We returned to the basement and I sat on the bed.

"Let me tell you about a vampire's strengths and weaknesses," Thorn said.

"Silver, crucifixes and fire?"

"Religious weapons do work, but it depends on the power of the vampire. It would only sting me, but others it would burn."

"Do you need inviting in places first?"

"No. And we have a reflection, which you have already worked out."

"Yes. I have seen you in front of the mirror trying on your outfits."

"We are just another species. We evolved differently from the norm and discovered the ability to turn other creatures into our image. A crude means of reproduction when necessary," she explained. "However, UV and silver do damage us, and decapitation works as well. I suppose a stake through the heart would kill us just like any creature. Fire only works on lesser vampires, some enjoy the flames," she said, grinning.

She pressed the button under the bed, and the weapons rack appeared from behind the big picture of the vampire and werewolf fighting. She walked over, grabbed a torch and a box with a knife in it.

"It is important you learn to recognise the pain from UV and silver to react correctly," she said.

I held out my hand for her to test on. She flicked the torch on and the light hit my hand. I braced myself for the searing flesh and smoke, but nothing happened. Thorn's face was puzzled, and she placed her own hand in front of it to check and the air filled with smoke. She flung the torch onto the bed and nursed her hand.

"Strange. Let us try again," she said and grabbed the torch and shone it over my hand. There was no reaction. I rolled up my sleeves and tried the UV on my arms, but there was no reaction.

"Let us try the silver," I said, smiling at this discovery.

"Okay. Open the box and try to pick it up."

I opened the box and hovered my finger above it for a few seconds, and then lowered it onto the silver. I pressed one finger against it. No reaction again. I picked it up in one hand, and there was no change. I swung it about in the air. Thorn backed off to avoid the blade and stood beside the bed, looking puzzled.

"I am immune," I said and laughed.

She frowned and eyed me like a curious puzzle. "Strange, I guess as you are only a temporary vampire, you haven't picked up our weaknesses but have kept our strengths. It will make you a formidable weapon."

She checked her watch. "We still had a few hours of darkness. Let's go out and test your powers."

"I agree. I need to go out and burn off this energy."

We drove around in the night together, sensing the humans and detecting their heartbeats glowing in the dark. The car in front, the driver was drunk; he thought randomly and sluggishly. A young man, sticking to the shadows, had just burgled some nearby houses. I detected sleeping people mostly, random blurred images from their dreams and thoughts and feelings firing around chaotically in the night.

As we drove on, we detected a large gathering in an empty warehouse. I focused on my abilities, and Thorn slowed down as feelings of fear and impending violence flashed across our minds from the people inside. It intrigued me. I wanted to understand what was happening, and Thorn seemed equally intrigued.

"Shall we?" she asked.

"Yes."

CHAPTER SEVENTEEN

Thorn hand-braked the car in the road, and the tyres screeched and smoked. I held on tight to the armrest as the car whipped around in the empty road and drove back through the smoke to the warehouse.

We cruised through the industrial estate, forcing our senses to home in on the strange set of signals. As we approached, the heartbeats became stronger and I could sense emotions of fear and violence from two different groups inside. We pulled up and sat outside.

"Close your eyes. Feel their emotions and listen to their thoughts," she said.

I copied her, closed my eyes and picked up their emotions, and the thoughts came in between the feelings. First, feelings of fear raced through my mind, followed by images of violent and sexual memories from a group inside. Images of men pinning them down, arms bruised from their grip, and stomachs and ribs hurting from punches inflicted to subdue them. Their limbs were restricted, and they were breathing hard through their noses, as their mouths were blocked, preventing them from screaming for help. I connected into a girl's thoughts as she struggled against her bonds. "We are never going to escape," she thought.

Images of a burly unshaven man approached, and he slapped her across the side of the face. Her mind went blank with face stinging, brain rattling and head bouncing off the floor. He shouted again as she lay crumpled, blood trickling out of her nose.

Next, I sensed the emotions of the violent group inside. I picked up feelings of the man who just hit the girl. His thoughts were full of anger. "Why don't these bloody girls learn to sit still?"

He looked down at her ragged blonde hair and cheeks blowing to breathe around the dirty rags stuffed and tied around her mouth. Her pale skin marked in dirty patches from the warehouse floor, teary blue eyes and blood trickling out of her nose. He looked at his watch and thought, "Still time to enjoy myself before the others arrive." His disgusting lust imaged her body and scared face, as he intended to take her, without her consent.

Thorn quickly got out of the car, flung her jacket into the seat and walked up to the side of the warehouse door. She beckoned me over to join her.

"Listen," she said.

My improved hearing picked up the conversation.

"How many girls do we have?" a man said.

"Ten, all ready for shipment," another man replied.

Thorn's eyes blazed red.

"Watch how it's done," she said, and then stood back and kicked the door flying off its hinges into the warehouse. She stepped through, and I followed on excited to see what Thorn could do in full battle rage.

A few dim light bulbs hung from long cords, masking the dust and grime that covered the warehouse floor. Ten girls, about my age, sat in a circle in the middle of the dirty floor, directly underneath one of the lights. They had dirty clothes, tear stained eyes, hands bound behind their backs and dirty rags gagged their mouths. I sensed them before seeing them, and I knew each of their thoughts. Their scents bombarded me with smells of dirt and sweat, and their fear intoxicated me. The sight of them tied up and gagged sparked the urge to feed. An easy meal.

The man I had seen earlier dragged the ragged blonde, with blood trickling out of her nose, to the back of the warehouse. The girls looked at us in the hope of salvation, and it reminded me of the look Giles gave me at the front gates of the school. Eyes stretched wide in fear, hoping someone would rescue them. They all looked at us, and they hoped we would offer that salvation.

The door had fired across the warehouse and skidded to a halt before the four men imprisoning the girls. They had jolted around and spotted us stepping inside, and then looked about for more people at the other exits at the opposite ends, left and right of where they stood. Their initial fears altered into feelings of anger at being disturbed by Thorn and I. Intentions of violence towards us filled their minds, and the adrenaline and testosterone raced through their bodies to combat the new threat. My urge to feed on the girls had been replaced with feelings of anger and aggression towards these men. Having experienced the memories and fears of the girls imprisoned, I felt like it had happened to me. I wanted revenge for having experienced those feelings as if I were one of the girls. Plus, they looked like they would provide a better hunt and a bigger meal.

"Who the hell are you?" the burly unshaven man shouted, dropping the girl with the bloodied nose to the floor. He signalled the others to get Thorn and joined them as they approached us.

I stepped back to allow Thorn to show off her skills. A slight smile appeared on her face, and her thoughts sounded in my head. "They are already dead."

"I am Thorn, and I have come to make you bleed."

They flicked out knives and drew out batons. They swung them about as they closed in. Thorn waited for them to get close enough, standing motionless and showing no emotion. They were steps away, batons coiled back and their sweaty stink burning my nostrils. Thorn unleashed her vampire rage; eyes glowing red, fangs cutting through her gums and claws ripping through the ends of her fingers. She roared, arching her back and head up in the air, with her fangs gleaming in the light. A primaeval shudder cascaded through their bodies as the sound resonated in their stomachs, triggering a pre-historic response to run, and they did run.

She leapt after the man who hit the girl, jumping high above his head and then down, leg extended onto his skull, smashing his face into the concrete floor. His head exploded like a melon, and she skidded in control on the blood, spinning around to face the remaining men. She pointed at a man running for the two main doors at the other end of the warehouse and darted after the other two men running in the opposite direction.

I sprinted after him, sensing his fear as he tried to escape. I ran past, stopped a couple of meters in front and faced him. The six-foot tall, fat man glared down and only saw a teenage boy. I relished the idea of taking him down and waited, as Thorn did, for him to get close enough first. I had plenty of pent up rage after Thorn killed me, and anger after hearing about the O'Keefe gang escaping justice. I would make sure these people didn't escape justice tonight. Vengeance for these girls would be immediate.

He ran again with baton coiled on his shoulder. I let the vampire rage take over, revealing fangs, claws and eyes burning bright red. I ducked his swipe and slashed my claws across his stomach. He stumbled to one side, dropped the baton and looked back at me. His eyes met my mutated features and the colour in his face drained away. He tried to run for the door again. I grabbed him by his arm, swung him around and around in a circle, lifting him off his feet and then firing him like a hammer into the wall of the building. He smashed into the wall and then laid crumpled, blood pouring from his nose and face, spluttering words as I walked over. I put my foot on his head and stamped. The skull cracked and an eyeball fired across the floor.

I walked back to Thorn, who had already killed the remaining two guards. One hung from the light fitting at the end of the warehouse, eyes gouged out and blood dripping to the floor. The other slumped against a blood-stained wall, throat ripped out but no blood on his clothes. Thorn smiled and his blood soaked in on her chin as she untied the girls. I sensed the girls' fear. The same as before, but now of Thorn and I.

I walked to the back of the group and untied the girl with the bloodied nose and ragged blonde hair. The images in her mind replayed of Thorn jumping high in the air, holding the guard and wrapping the electric cord from the light around his neck. I snipped the cloth around her arms with one of my claws, and she grabbed the gag from around her mouth and slung it across the floor.

"Thank you," she said, looking straight into my mutated eyes.

I winked and gave a little smile, and a friend grabbed her by the arm and dragged her to the exit.

The main warehouse doors opened at the end where I had killed the guard, and in drove three old and battered white vans. I focused in on the men sat in the front seats, their emotions and senses altered by the sight of their prisoners running off and the mutilated bodies of the four guards. They drove on quickly, with the passengers reaching for weapons and shouting at each other.

I pushed my senses past them and into the back of the vans and sensed more girls tied and gagged. Their emotions and thoughts replicating what I had detected earlier in the girls now escaping through the exit. They bounced along in total darkness in the back of the van, struggling to breathe and reliving horrible memories from their kidnappings.

The drivers slammed on their brakes, and the doors burst open as nine rough and angry men piled out with weapons in hand: baseball bats, knives and one man dressed in a shiny grey suit holding a gun.

The suited man aimed. I dropped to one knee, pulling my pistol out of the back of my trousers and fired. My vampire powers allowed me to focus in on my target, and I moved quicker than he anticipated. The bullet travelled along its perfect trajectory straight into his eye and bursting out the back of his head, smashing the windscreen on the van behind. He flew back onto the floor, his gun sliding out of his hand and under the van. They froze in fear.

"No guns," Thorn shouted.

I threw it on the warehouse floor, but kept the bullets and placed them into my pocket.

The rest of the men eyed us. They looked down the warehouse and pointed to the guard swinging from the ceiling. Their surprise turned to anger, and they charged towards us, yelling with weapons at the ready.

Thorn walked to my side, and we faced the gang together as a team. Thorn looked at me and smiled with her eyes burning red.

"Jackpot," she said, grinning.

"We're the good guys?" I asked.

"Why not?"

We exchanged thoughts for a few seconds and devised a plan. We didn't wait for them this time, and charged at them in full battle rage; vampire weapons brandished and bodies full of blood lust.

We jumped high into the air and then pierced down with our claws out wide slashing into a few either side. They scattered as our claws ripped through and injured three of their number. The others panicked at the sight of their fallen friends and monstrous features on our faces. They fled to the exits, but we covered their escape paths, forcing them to fight.

I went for the one running back to the door. I grabbed his arm and then swung him back into a man charging at me, knocking him over like a skittle.

At the far end, two girls had stopped and watched the battle. The ragged blonde haired girl and friend that had helped her up. They weren't scared anymore but angry. One man jumped back to his feet and ran off to the far end towards the two girls. The other ran towards me, brandishing a knife and attacked.

I slipped inside the stabbing action and grabbed his arm with one hand, twisted it around so the palm faced upwards and elbow joint faced downwards. I smacked my other open hand through the elbow joint breaking his arm. The knife dropped, and he fell to the floor clutching his arm and screaming in agony. I stepped in and broke his neck.

The two girls at the other end hadn't run upon seeing the man approaching, but had picked up a knife and baton from their previous captors. They blocked the exit. He punched the ragged blonde's friend hard, knocking her to the floor, and then the blonde girl stepped in and stabbed his stomach. He pushed her aside and staggered onwards. I picked up a dropped knife, tunnelled my vision and threw it spinning through the air, arching down and hitting him on the side of his back. He tripped and fell by the door, but still tried to get up and crawl away.

The girl with the baton clambered back to her feet. She carried a nasty bruise on her face. She jumped onto his back, hitting him as hard as she could over the head. The ragged blonde came back around the side, pulled out the knife in his back and repeatedly stabbed it in his stomach. He stopped moving and slumped, blood spilling out over the dirty warehouse floor.

I finished off another, slicing his throat open in a spinning back claw movement. Thorn finished the last opponent but one. I entertained Thorn and me for a bit with the last opponent we had cornered. Thorn enjoyed the spectacle and eventually signalled me to finish.

The girls waited as we walked back down the warehouse. The blonde girl stood still while the other held her hand, pulling and pleading with her to leave. They both feared us and watched as we approached, blood soaking into our skin, fangs retracting, eyes changing back to normal in a blink and claws sliding back into our fingers. The muscles on our faces relaxed, losing their contorted aggressive features, and our flesh resumed its normal colour from its aggressive sick grey. Thorn smiled as we approached, and I sensed her pushing comforting thoughts into their minds.

"Calm, relax."

The girls followed the instructions without conscious agreement and relaxed. The blonde's friend stopped talking and pulling on her hand and smiled back at us. I already knew from their thoughts they had been through an unimaginable hell. The suffering I felt was nothing compared to what they had been through.

We stood in front of them, and we both smiled. I copied Thorn, pushing relaxing thoughts into their minds.

"We want to join you. Make us one of you," the blonde one pleaded.

"What are your names?" Thorn asked.

"Annabel and Lucinda," she said, and pointed to herself first and then to Lucinda.

"No, Annabel, you can't, but I can help you."

"Please, I don't want to be scared anymore, I want revenge on these people."

"I know, we understand. There are more important things for you to do in your life," Thorn said.

"We have nowhere else to go. We are both homeless. Someone else will get us eventually."

"Go and release the other girls from those vans. I will call the police to come and help you. Then when you are done, go to this address," Thorn said and pulled out a business card from her wallet. "Tell them Tracy Horn sent you. The lady there, Miss Jones, will look after you."

The girls looked at Thorn, and I sensed they wanted more. "That's the offer. Take it or leave it," Thorn said and stared at them with the card held out.

Annabel stared at Thorn for a moment and Lucinda whispered, "Take it."

"Thank you," Annabel said and took the card.

"You will hear from us again one day," Thorn said.

We headed out the doors, stepping over the dead body of the guard the girls had killed. I looked around one last time at the bodies of the men scattered around the warehouse floor, hanging from the ceiling still dripping with blood, limbs bleeding on the bonnets of the vans and bloody footprints stamped across the floor. I couldn't believe we had done this in such a short space of time.

We got back in the car, and I turned to talk to Thorn about the girls.

"I have only room for one apprentice. Besides, it is always important to have connections and build favours. Those girls may be of use to us one day," she said.

"Tracy Horn?" I asked.

"Yes, T. Horn, Thorn," she replied, and I got the meaning. "Miss Jones will find them places to stay, get them educated and integrated back into society. They will be of use to us then. Helping us to hide and move through time unnoticed."

There was always an angle, a strategy.

"It will be light soon. We must get back," she said.

She fired up the engine and spun the car out of the warehouse parking. I saw the two girls in the rear-view mirror staring at us as we left, still holding the card Thorn had given them. I wondered if we would see them again as we burned back down the road towards home.

"When you first entered the warehouse, what were your thoughts towards the girls?" Thorn asked as we drove home.

I didn't lie. There was no point.

"I wanted to feed on them. Their fear was exciting."

"What stopped you?" she asked.

"The men, their aggression and violent thoughts washed over those feelings and took away my attention."

"Yes. Even I felt the pull of those girls tied and gagged as an easy meal. Be aware of the power the thirst has over us. If you understand it, you can use it to good effect," she said.

"I relived those girls' memories and wanted revenge as if it had happened to me."

"Well done, using their memories and emotions to fuel you. Putting yourself in their shoes instead is a good idea."

I was learning more and beginning to understand the life of a vampire was far from simple.

We returned before light, happy and full. Thorn dragged me hand-in-hand down the stairs to get me back before my vampire power wore off. I had caught her watching me fighting the last gang member, licking her lips with one hip dropped, and I sensed her passion being triggered. I played with him a bit in front of Thorn to show off my powers and to increase her desire.

'Finish it,' she had pushed the thought into my mind.

I had allowed him to charge at me one more time, and stepped in and snapped his neck to finish it before we headed off and talked to Annabel and Lucinda. I guessed Thorn hadn't been with another vampire for some time, and she wanted to spend my last vampire moments locked together in the safety of her house.

My vampire instincts extended into this realm as well. Although not experienced, an animal vampire urge overrode my human inhibitions as Thorn and I tore into each other fighting for dominance, taking it in turns to take the lead. Vampire on vampire lovemaking was a whole new game for me to learn.

Afterwards, I watched Thorn fall asleep. She looked so peaceful and happy and entirely different from the sad and lonely woman I had seen in the prison cell all those weeks ago. Despite her killing me tonight, I, Night Jonathan, had fallen in love with her. It wasn't just her powers tricking me. She had given me a new lease of life. It was the most exciting time of my life, and I wished the night could go on forever. I hated the idea of the coming daytime, in fear of what Day Jonathan would think and the plans he was hatching.

I decided not to waste any of the formula and took a trip out into the daylight. I ambled off to the park with a smile and spring in my step, and I sat on a cold park bench as the morning sun lit up the grass and a mist rose up. The formula wore off, and as it did my daytime self, Day Jonathan, took control.

"You've been lucky to survive tonight. She killed you," Day Jonathan said.

"I know but we made it through stronger than before," I, Night Jonathan, replied.

"Scarlett still wants us back. There is a way home after all."

"So what? She betrayed us, remember. We have Thorn now."

"Thorn will kill us eventually. We are being used for something," I, Day Jonathan, said as my personality shifted.

"No, we have a deal. I love her," he exclaimed.

"Don't be stupid, it's her powers. You don't realise what you are saying," I said with the formula drifting away and Night Jonathan with it, and my normal human senses returning.

"I ... I ..." Night Jonathan tried to say, but he disappeared as the formula dispersed, and my body changed back to normal again.

I had transformed back to Day Jonathan again, free with my own thoughts. Looking back over the night's events, I realised I only just escaped death at Thorn's hands. I was lucky to be alive. It was the scariest time of my life. Saving the girls had been a good thing to do, but I had killed people. Maybe there was a better way. Maybe I could still help people like that, wherever I ended up, without killing.

Also, Scarlett wanted me back and offered me a way out, and those words still echoed in my head during the day. Could there really be a way back? It was what I wanted during those daylight hours. Yet, I owed Thorn so much. We had a deal, but at times, it felt more like a pact with the devil. Last night it was a mixture of fun and fear with Thorn, but that was a true reflection, although more extreme than most nights with her. Thorn had never betrayed me. She had only ever kept to her word. Even if it hurt, I was becoming stronger under her guidance.

I needed time to think about going home to a normal life. Maybe it wasn't just a fantasy. To protect Scarlett in the meantime, I had to forget her. If I dwelled on her for too long, Thorn might detect my thoughts and both of us would be dead. Once we had finished with Barry, I could sneak out and get away from Thorn during the day and find my way back to Scarlett.

Maybe it wasn't too late to have a normal life. I just needed to follow the plan I had been building as Day Jonathan, and I hoped that Night Jonathan would survive long enough to make it through or not betray us to Thorn.

CHAPTER EIGHTEEN

From my last change, the vampire power lasted longer, and I had greater control over it being able to change in and out quickly. I felt the hypnotic powers and psychic abilities on the last injection, pushing my thoughts into the minds of Annabel and Lucinda.

Once the power had gone, I'd grown again, stronger, faster, taller and more handsome as well. My fighting instinct seemed to have improved. I could feel the moves and actions I should take when back in my human body. It had pushed the boundaries of my human form, which never fully returned to normal again afterwards, like the elastic on a rubber band stretched too far. I waited to see if this included psychic abilities, but I was happy with my new powers in vampire and human form.

A couple of days after seeing Scarlett and fighting in the warehouse, I was Day Jonathan and had continued putting energy into my escape plan. I had bought a silver knife, stuffed it deep into my rucksack and counted the remaining change. I walked around the corner to a phone shop and bought the cheapest mobile I could find with ten pounds worth of credit, and I test called it to ensure it was working. I headed back to the house, hid my escape kit in the loft and carried on with my vampire training.

At night, I had changed back to Night Jonathan again. I drove us back from one of Thorn's hunting grounds. Thorn shuffled in her seat and checked her mobile phone.

"You can always drink from me. I am sure I can spare a pint of blood," I said.

"Thank you, but no. You need your strength. I have some bottled blood in the fridge at home. I thought this might happen. The police and Hunters are making it impossible to feed."

"Are you sure they were Hunters or police?" I said.

"Of course, I am sure. I heard their thoughts. They have everywhere covered. We have to move."

"But what about Barry?"

"His house is too heavily guarded. They are waiting for us. It's a trap. The video he has is no longer a threat. The Hunters would have taken it. They don't want the public to know we exist."

"So we just forget about Barry?"

"No. But he can wait for your revenge. In the meantime, we should look elsewhere to continue your training and for me to get a feed."

"Where should we go? Can we go abroad?" I said.

She stared out the window and then back at her phone. "Tell me about Leeds."

"It's a city in Yorkshire, England."

"Ha ha, hilarious, you know what I mean. Tell me about your life in Leeds. Tell me about Giles and the car accident."

I gripped hard on the steering wheel and said nothing.

"Jon, tell me what happened in Leeds. It is obviously important. Scarlett mentioned a court case. I can just read your mind if I wanted. You are probably thinking about it right now. You can just tell me instead."

"I don't want to talk about it. Go ahead and read my mind. I will run through the memories."

"Okay. Just play it out in your mind and I will hear, see and feel all of it, as if it was me."

I started at the beginning outside the school with the gang hassling Giles. I played it from the car crash, the bullying at school and the brick through the window until the move to London.

She sat in silence with her eyes closed, and then her phone beeped. She opened her eyes.

"You feel guilty about leaving him with the gang. Also, you fear the gang, even though you have the vampire formula and me at your side."

"Yes. They bullied me for years. I can't even picture them without feeling scared."

"This is perfect."

"Thanks. Perfect that I am still terrified of the school bullies."

"Yes. Visiting Leeds and taking revenge will be a perfect way to move your training forward."

"Maybe another time when I have finished my training."

"Your training is to face your fears. We go to Leeds tomorrow night. That beep on my phone was the hotel confirmation. No arguments." I said nothing, but I could picture Patrick's scared face when I turned into a vampire in front of him.

The next evening, Thorn awoke an hour before darkness fell. We packed our bags and jumped into the car as soon as the sun dipped below the horizon. We drove up the motorway. The drive only took a few hours and as it was wintertime, the sunset had been early. We arrived at a posh hotel in the middle of the city centre. We parked underground and got the lift to the reception. Thorn booked us in and a man showed us to an elevator and hit the button for the top floor. We rode up, looking out the window into the city centre as we rose above it all.

The lift stopped and the doors slid apart. "The Penthouse suite madam. The whole top floor is yours."

The penthouse was a massive room with a king-sized bed, sofas, large mahogany table, marbled bathroom suite and balcony looking over the city. I toured the room, amazed by its luxury, and realised this was another benefit of life with Thorn.

I walked out onto the balcony, watching the city below and felt excited about being back in Leeds. The sounds of the city rose up from the ground, with cars and buses navigating around the streets. People marched along in the cold through the illuminated maze of pathways and roads, looking for shelter in their favourite hangouts. The city bustled as it got into the full swing of a big Saturday night.

Thorn had a plan for tomorrow night of touring the places and events of my past, to face my fears and confront them as part of my training, but that was tomorrow night. Tonight we were going out into the city to have some fun. I had never been out in the city at night as I was too scared, and I'd never imagined I would until I was a lot older.

On the way up in the car, I talked to Thorn about all the places I wanted to visit and all the things I wanted to do. I knew of all the trendy spots, as I had heard about them second-hand at school or read about them on social networking sites, but Thorn knew of better places.

She joined me on the balcony and looked out over the city.

"Nice view," I said.

"Yes, you should see it as I see it," she replied.

I imagined all the smells, colours and emotions flowing through her as she plugged into the city with her vampire senses.

"I like the room."

"It will do," she said, as the breeze flapped her raven hair across her face.

"Where does all your money come from?" I asked.

"Well, I have had a lot of years to save up. Compound interest is a marvellous thing. Being able to read minds is useful. I am especially good at poker and getting inside tips on the stock market as well. The problem isn't getting the money. It's getting rid of it. I can't afford to have too much money in one name, as it generates too many questions. I give a lot to charity," she said.

I laughed. The idea of a vampire giving money away to charity sounded ridiculous.

"I know it's a strange idea. It's not from the goodness of my heart, but purely practical. It buys favours and builds my other identities and networking contacts. I invest in companies conducting research as well. Anything that could give me an advantage. Money isn't the point, it's all about power."

"Power over whom?"

"Over those who wish to destroy me and my kind," she answered.

"The Hunters?"

"Yes, and others. But the time for a history lesson is after you have completed your training. For now, I need to keep you and the needles a secret."

I had pressed the question on other vampires and her history before but had always been rebuffed.

"Why?" I asked again, looking around at her, feeling braver now we had spent time together.

She gazed into the distance and closed her eyes, letting the cold air wash over her. I sensed memories flashing through her mind. Images of fire and smoke blazing around, as battles against armoured knights raged. Swords cutting through the smoke as screams and roars engulfed the air. Vampires fighting the knights and then trying to escape into the darkness. Vampires like her glowing and passionate, and others dark, half-dead, and decaying in the shadows. Her memories jumped back to other battles, showing glimpses of giant wings beating in the air and knights charging in with red crosses emblazoned on their tunics. The images moved around to reveal the source of the wings. The images blackened, cutting off the final reveal, as she forced me out of her mind. She turned around and frowned.

"You are getting stronger. Psychic powers as well. I must be more careful around you," she said, a little perturbed.

"Sorry, I didn't mean to. It just sort of happens sometimes," I said, hoping I hadn't crossed the line.

"So the other powers remain with you afterwards as well, not just the physical strengths?"

I hadn't mentioned it before; I was trying to keep it a secret. My hidden ace in the pack, but the secret was blown.

"Yes. A little of the power I had as a vampire remains. My powers seem to improve upon every needle, and a residual amount remains and grows each time," I confessed.

"Interesting, you are becoming more fascinating."

She turned and held both my hands, so we were face-to-face. "I will tell all eventually, but first I must be sure you are ready. You must complete the training."

Her bright sky eyes shone and she smiled. Her mist rose around us, finishing the conversation.

"Let's party," she said and walked back through the door into the penthouse room, pulling me behind her.

CHAPTER NINETEEN

After a restful sleep from a night out in the city, I woke with the last of the light fading around the edges of the curtains, giving the room a dim covering. Thorn lay asleep beside me, but it wouldn't be long before she woke. I was Day Jonathan and thoughts crossed my mind of pulling the curtains back and exposing her to the UV light. I could kill her and be free to be with Scarlett again. Free from the fears that Thorn would kill me or get me killed. As the night came, I could sense Thorn awakening, and I could feel Night Jonathan taking over.

"Let's open the curtains and kill her," I, Day Jonathan, said.

"Why? You have a deal, and she is keeping it," he, Night Jonathan, replied.

"But I was wrong to make that deal. It was a deal you made," I said.

"We both wanted it. Don't pretend you haven't been happy with your new strength and abilities."

"I am, but it's gone far enough. Who knows what she has planned tonight," Day Jonathan said, his voice fading with the light dwindling around the corners of the curtains.

"Well, hopefully some excitement and blood," I, Night Jonathan, said.

"More blood on your hands. How can you sleep?"

"Easy, in the knowledge I am safe, and no one can hurt me anymore. This is what we both wanted. You just don't have the strength to admit it and see it through," I said.

"It's not that simple," he said, his voice nearly a whisper.

"Why not," I said, and grinned, as I, Night Jonathan, took control once more. "Last night was great being out in the city. A place we never thought we could go. Thorn has given us so much. You need to trust her, as she trusts us," I, Night Jonathan, said, as Day Jonathan diminished again.

Darkness had fallen, and Thorn woke up. She sat up in bed, and we kissed as the sheet fell away from her body, revealing her perfect figure.

"It will be a good night. I can sense it," she said and padded off to the shower room to get ready.

I switched on the news as Thorn showered. It played in the background, and I considered if I would be on the news in a couple of nights after our visit.

Thorn came back and dressed to get attention on the tour of the city, short tartan kilt skirt, white high heels and tiny white crop top. I went to ask her if she was really going out dressed like that when she looked at me with her eyebrows raised.

"Yes, I am."

I hated it when she read my mind.

Thorn insisted I wore my new clothes: designer blue pre-roughed up jeans, Ducati retro 50s black leather jacket, grey tight surfing t-shirt and brown suede boots. I felt good in the new clothes, and as a couple, we were an unusual sight with Thorn dressed as if on a night out clubbing. She looked a lot older than me, more than people realised. In fact, she was older than everyone. I looked like her young toy boy. I could tell by the hotel staff's reaction and snippets of their thoughts, they assumed I had lots of money to have a woman like Thorn. They were surprised when she paid for the room and the food in the restaurant using her special platinum credit card. They spoke to Thorn with deference and respect on their return, having previously ignored her because of her clothes and assumption that I had the money. As I finished my steak and chips, a couple of waitresses gathered in a corner and looked over at us.

Thorn smiled at me. "They can't decide on our relationship. They thought I was some sort of trophy girlfriend. Now they think I am a sugar mummy, corrupting some poor young boy," she laughed.

"You are, aren't you?" I laughed back.

Thorn frowned at me for a moment, and I froze with panic at my joke gone wrong.

"Yes, I am!" she said and laughed again as she knocked back her vodka and tonic.

We drove to my old house in the quiet cul-de-sac I had lived in all my life before London. The windows had been boarded up, with new red writing across them. "Run Grass." The For Sale sign looked battered and wasted as long as the attacks continued. Dad hadn't been able to sell the house, and it was causing him financial issues with a mortgage and rent to pay.

I remembered all the years I spent in the house with just Dad and me. It was better when I was younger, as we had live-in help to look after me. Dad decided I was old enough at fourteen years old to take myself to school and to take care of myself while he worked. The last few years had been lonely. Giles helped me through it, and I had abandoned him at his time of need. I remembered the happy times, Dad teaching me to ride my bike and playing in the back garden.

And I remembered the bad times, living in fear after the accident and as a home alone fourteen-year-old. Dad devoted himself to work when I reached fourteen by taking on his new night time project, which I guessed was connected to Thorn, but she had always been based in London. His work was still a mystery, and I would like to get some answers someday. I explained it all to Thorn as we sat outside, and she soaked it in, looking at the house and reliving my memories as I played them out in my mind.

We drove on to my old school, "St Teresa's," and I stood at the front gates looking at the names and faces scratched in the red paint. I took out a black permanent marker and wrote on the square railings on the gate.

"Jonathan Harper returned." I added in the date next to it.

I hoped someone would see it upon returning to school, and it would be a talking point. I looked through the gates into the courtyard and the road snaking around the side to the car park at the back. My memory relived finding Giles surrounded by the O'Keefe's gang, with his eyes bulging in fear as he looked for salvation. I remembered Liam scaring me off and punching me in the stomach. I then walked around the corner, trying to justify my cowardice as tactics.

I imagined how different life would have been if I hadn't had been scared off but stood my ground and tried to help. Or if one teacher, like Mr May, or one parent had done something other than look away.

Maybe the car accident could have been avoided, and Giles and I would still be friends. I may have still been living in Leeds but could have still been living in fear. Maybe I was better off that it did all happen, else I would have never met Thorn, but I would never have been mugged by Barry and betrayed by Scarlett either.

Yet, there were no guarantees life would have been better in Leeds or London. I had to make the best of my present situation. However, I still wanted revenge on all those that had done me wrong: Barry, O'Keefes, Mr May and Scarlett. I would have revenge on all of them. Yes, even Scarlett had to answer for betraying me, just as I would need to answer to Giles. As the weeks had worn on and I lived more of my life as Night Jonathan, and my desire for vengeance had become stronger.

Thorn looked around for a bit and listened as I explained the events in detail. I could tell she was reliving those memories and emotions as I said it. I held myself together as sadness welled up from all the years of fear I suffered at school and that fateful day of the accident. She held my hand as I explained.

"They can't hurt you anymore," she said as we hugged, "remember what you have become. You have a rare opportunity to put things right."

I nodded, and I knew without any psychic abilities what she had planned for the night.

"Good, now where do they live?" she asked, standing back and pressing the car key fob, making the car lights flash and the locks clunk into place.

I wasn't particularly keen on walking into that place at night, as the old fears were too strong to quash, but she wasn't taking no for an answer, so I pointed in the right direction. Thorn walked on to the estate, putting on a terrific show, swaying her hips back and forth as if she belonged on a catwalk. I knew her game, as she had done this before. It was her way of hunting. She didn't go to find her prey; she got them to find her. She was the honey and the trap. We got the attention she desired as we walked through the estate. Cars beeped, and young men leered out of the windows, and a few local youths wolf-whistled. Thorn enjoyed the attention and blew kisses at them, trying to provoke them into fatal action.

The further we walked into the estate, the more uncomfortable I felt. The houses got more run down, windows broken and boarded up. Litter on the streets blew about from the abandoned garbage. I would have never walked around here day or night. My muscles tensed up and stomach tightened, and I looked down at the floor as we walked, trying to avoid everyone's gaze. Thorn stopped, grabbed my shoulder and I looked up. Her eyes flashed red, and she bared her fangs for a second. I remembered whom I was walking with and pulled myself upright. We carried on deeper into the hunting ground. I loved it when she read my mind.

As we turned onto another road, I recognised it as the place the accident happened. I could even find the exact spot and pointed it out to Thorn. I remembered Liam catapulting over the car and his motionless body behind it. I remembered opening the door, being sick and running off, as scared of what would happen next. And I was right to be scared, as they came after us, driving Giles to suicide, and I would have been next if it hadn't been for my Dad's work.

As Thorn was reliving my memories, a gang of three lads came around the corner. Thorn caught their attention, and they stopped and stared. She held their gaze and strutted towards them, giving it everything to fuel their desires. They approached full of swagger and bluff, pulling their hoodies down, and I recognised one of the lads from the gang, Dave. He acted as Patrick's right-hand man in school, always there to serve as the extra muscle and had bullied Giles and me in the past. Dave's face pulled a quizzical look as he recognised me. He had shaven his ginger hair and sported a piercing in his eyebrow. His face pale and spot covered as always.

"Jon?"

"Yeah," I said, standing up straight.

"Hardly recognise you, especially not here."

"Well, just showing my girlfriend around."

Thorn stood next to me, hugging my arm and smiling at Dave, acting the part to perfection.

He looked surprised.

"Really? Why here?" he asked.

"I want to find the O'Keefe's house," Thorn answered.

"Why would you want to find them for?" Dave asked.

"I have a deal for them," Thorn said.

"Not going to happen, sweetheart. Now run along and put some clothes on."

"Come on, Dave, why don't you tell us?" I asked, playing along with Thorn's game.

"You've some guts all of a sudden. Not that long ago you did everything you could to hide from us. Even left your mate to fend for himself. Well, I have news for you. The police and schools have better things to do than watch us," Dave said, and paced back and forth as he spoke.

"We found those little grasses that came after us. You had better leave now. No one has forgotten your part in what happened to Liam. Even though you were too scared to come to the trial."

I couldn't be bothered to explain why I wasn't at the trial.

"Not going to beat me up first?" I asked, as I sensed something was missing. They usually just hit first.

"I have heard things about you. Police and others have been around here asking questions about you. We thought at first that they were blaming us for your disappearance. But no, they wanted to catch you for some murders in London."

"Really," I said, happy that I had a reputation.

"Yeah, so go on leave. I have better things to do," Dave said and walked backwards, keeping his eyes on us.

Even without the remnant vampire power, I could tell he feared us and was suspicious of me being back in Leeds.

"I want the O'Keefe's address, and I want it now," Thorn shouted.

She let go of my arm and stood legs apart, hand on hips and face frowning.

"Tell your whore to shut up," Dave shouted back.

I placed my hand across Thorn's chest to hold her still. I didn't need to be psychic to know what she wanted to do. I decided to do Dave a favour. He wouldn't thank me for it, but it would save his life and those of his friends. I could just let Thorn kill them, but I hated him and something inside just snapped. I didn't need to let the anger build to fuel my actions. As soon as I saw him, I wanted to punch his stupid spotty face. I walked over.

"Oh, big man are you? Come on then," Dave called me forward with his hands and then squeezed them into fists.

He swung first. I parried and returned a punch, and he staggered back into his two friends. He swung another fist, and I dived back and followed up with a roundhouse kick across his thigh, dropping him to one knee.

The other two advanced forwards. I front kicked the closest in the stomach, flinging him backwards and tumbling along the pavement. The other one caught me with a blow to the side of the head, and I rocked backwards but stayed on my feet. I turned and jumped back to gain some space. He came again, and I lunged forwards grabbing him around the neck with both hands locked behind his head. I sprung a flurry of knees into his ribs while pulling him down onto them.

Dave got back to his feet, and the second friend picked himself up as well. The one I held tried to drop out of my grasp, and I let him drop his head to meet a right knee full force into his face. He collapsed to the floor, and I jumped one-footed on his back and flew forward with another knee and elbow out in front of me, straight into Dave's oncoming charge. The force of my attack broke through his feeble block and smashed him to the floor. The third one froze as I piled through Dave, and then he turned and ran back down the road. I knelt down, grabbed Dave by the head and pulled back my fist ready to continue.

"Where do they live?" I shouted.

I sensed Thorn's thoughts in my head. "Good, you are learning."

I smiled to myself, and I soaked in my feelings of triumph and victory. This was the first time I had ever won a fight, and it was against my old tormentor. I was enjoying my newly found strength in my human form. Vengeance felt great.

CHAPTER TWENTY

The time hit midnight as we stood in front of a terraced house with lights flashing in the downstairs window. Accompanying the lights, screaming and moaning were coming from the TV. Above the noise of the TV, laughing and shouting joined in. The streets were deserted, and the lights above us flickered on and off every ten seconds.

I stared at the front door, preparing myself. I rehearsed it in my mind: across the path, through the assorted junk and rubbish dumped outside, around the weatherworn discarded sofa and smash through the front door, and then into the TV room.

Thorn looked at me. "You know what to do?"

"Yes."

I twitched with nervous excitement. I would have more control this time around to savour their destruction and fear. Thorn pulled the needle out of her pocket and prepared it by pushing it down and tapping it to force the air out.

"Remember to pass me some meat once inside," she said as I rolled up my sleeve.

"I will remember, Thorn," I said, and looked away to prepare for the injection.

"Look at it, Jon. You must face your fears," she said, waiting for me to turn back and look at the needle.

I did, and she plunged it into my skin and pushed down the syringe, forcing the formula into my bloodstream. I waited for the power to come and the pain of my body changing, knowing it was the precursor to immense power. The formula streamed around my body, my heart racing, my blood burning up. I felt faint and red hot as my body transformed, driving it to its limits. My heart seized and legs buckled, but Thorn caught me.

The white light returned and the familiar accompanying face and voice. But, as before, death didn't last and I jolted back into my new vampire body. I stabilised and Thorn helped me to stand. I took a deep breath and soaked in the new scenery, as can only be seen and sensed by a vampire. The scent in the air, the glow of bodies and hearing their thoughts.

Thorn wrapped her arms around my neck and kissed me.

"Go now, my darling, relive your anger and fulfil your revenge. Bathe in your rage and then enjoy their fear and destruction."

My memory flashed back to those dark days in Leeds, and the sickening fear of an unknown attack. The constant feeling of being on edge. The image of poor Giles in the cloakroom on that last day in school still haunted me. The hate in his eyes as the tears streamed down his face, and then he attacked me, his best friend. Worst of all, the ever-present guilt I felt by walking away from those front gates and then allowing my Dad to make me abandon my friendship.

I let the guilt and anger for them escaping justice at the trial join in with the other emotions. The anger and rage built up, and I waited for its strength to push against my barriers of self-control. When it reached a climactic point, I released the barriers and let it flood through my body, soaking it in power, triggering the full strength and rage of the vampire within. It was enough. I blazed across the street, jumped the discarded weather-torn sofa and smashed straight through the front door into their house.

I burst into the smoke-filled room, with the TV the only light, which flashed its images across the walls and onto the four men watching it: the O'Keefe's father, Liam in his wheelchair, Patrick, and a friend from the gang. They were watching a torture porn film, showing a young woman in ripped nightclothes tied to a chair and a smiling man approaching with a spinning drill.

The father's stomach bulged out of his grubby white vest, straining at the buttons on his dirty blue jeans. Tattoos of barbed wire spiralled down his left shoulder to his forearm. On the other arm, the words, "Fighting Irish," tattooed in black and green across his bicep. He had some hair at the sides of his bald head pulled into a ratty black and grey ponytail.

Patrick and Liam were just as I remembered them. Patrick had short black hair and a greasy freckled pale face. Liam's face hardened, stubbled and depressed. They wore tracksuit tops, jeans and fancy new trainers. Patrick had a long rolled up joint in his hand and coughed out smoke on my entrance. The friend slumped on the sofa in a large green parker jacket, jeans and heavy-duty black boots.

They all had a can of drink in their hands, which they were putting down after being alerted by the noise of the front door. I faced them, blocking the light of the TV.

I knew what I wanted to do. I pictured myself turning their house into a blood bath in a terrifying blur of claws and fangs, but I controlled my instincts to kill and drink this time around. I decided to enjoy myself first. My face contorted, eyes burning red and fangs showing. I snarled and growled at them, and I sensed their building fear and panic as a trembling through their entire bodies. I felt it paralyse them into their stain-ridden paisley chairs. I stared at them one by one as I showed them my vampire face and snarled at them from the bottom of my guts. They looked around at each other in a panic, waiting for one of the others to do something, waiting for someone to take the lead.

I changed things about and reverted to my human face. They stopped sinking into their chairs in an attempt to escape and stood up and stared at me.

"It's Jonathan, Giles' friend. The one who disappeared. The one the police have been asking about," Patrick said.

I was surprised he recognised me.

"Yeah, he is," Liam replied.

Their fear started fading away now that they had sight of a kid they used to bully. Their confidence grew as I appeared in human form again, and they crept forward. The fear flipped to anger; the muscles in their arms tensed and white knuckles showed as they squeezed their fists ready to fight.

"Nice special effects, kid," the father said. "What next, a rabbit from a hat?"

They moved forward, looking at each other for reassurance.

"No, I am here for vengeance. I have a deal for you, a chance to understand the game of consequences." I paused. "You must choose which two of you will live and which two must die."

They stopped moving and again glanced around at each other.

"Or you all die," I said.

They looked at each other again. The boys all stared at the father, who laughed and flicked back his ratty ponytail. He still thought this was some kind of act.

"You made my life and Giles' hell. You bullied and beat and stole from us. Do you not have anything to say? No words to plea for your lives?" I asked.

"Don't make us laugh. You're just a stupid little child. This is just a trick, some fancy makeup and special effects. I couldn't give a toss about you and your friends. You paralysed my lad. It's the law of the jungle around here. Survival of the fittest. At least we don't have to go looking for you anymore. We can finish it here. No beating for you, a nice shallow grave in the woods instead," the father said and stepped forward.

"Good. Survive this."

I flew forward like a hammer into the father, breaking his ribs, and he flew through the air, getting wrapped up in the curtains and smashing through the windowpanes. He cleared the assorted debris left to rot in the garden and skidded to a halt at the feet of Thorn.

She ripped off the curtains.

"Breakfast."

She grabbed him by the ponytail, stared into his eyes, and said in a pretend sympathetic voice, "This is going to hurt a lot, darling," and offered a sad smile to accompany it.

She brandished her fangs and tore into his neck. He screamed as she drained his blood. I turned back and kicked through the knee of Patrick, breaking his leg. He crashed to the floor, and I added a slash of claws across his stomach to make sure he couldn't move. Patrick fell to the floor, grabbing his leg and stomach, trying to stem the flow of blood.

The friend ran to the door, and I leapt across and grabbed his arm, wrenching it from its socket. Blood spilt out onto the floor, and his screams of pain joined in with those from the TV and those from Patrick. I retracted my claws and hammered in a series of punches into his ribs, hearing each rib crack and break as it hit. Each hit accompanied by a shout of agony as the blows landed. He slumped to the floor.

Pain shot through my leg. A knife stuck out of it, and Liam was in his wheelchair next to me. I flung him across the room into the high, far corner.

The friend rolled in agony on the floor, pulling himself along to escape. I crouched over him, repeatedly punching him in the head until brains and blood discoloured the already filthy carpet and furniture.

Patrick's screaming gained my focus, and I strolled back over, savouring the moment and revelling in my revenge for all those years of bullying I suffered.

"Patrick, time to die."

I crouched down in front of him, and he tried to punch me, but I barely noticed in my vampire form. A loud and raucous laugh erupted from me at his pathetic attempt to fight back. I flicked open one claw and pushed back his head, exposing his neck.

"Go to hell," he screamed.

"Been there. It was being at school with you," I answered, and flicked my claw across his throat, slitting it and leaving a line of blood that opened up his neck.

He tried to speak as the blood poured from his neck but just spluttered blood out of his mouth instead.

I leant down to his ear.

"Justice at last. You took so much from me, but I have taken your life and your father's. Your mother and sisters will be next, and I will enjoy it,"

I said.

He flung his arms about to no effect and tears poured from his eyes, as the realisation of my total vengeance became real. His life slipped away as he struggled. I stood up and watched him die, and I felt relief from those long years of bullying and guilt from Giles' suicide.

The lights in the room flashed as the TV blared out its own screams and unsavoury noises, as the torture porn in the background reached its climax in parallel.

I walked back to Liam, who lay curled up in the corner of the room next to his broken wheelchair. I knelt down and whispered gently into his ear.

"Consequences. Everything has consequences. I am the physical manifestation of your actions. I am your consequence."

I realised someone was missing.

"Where is Kieran?" I asked.

Liam answered stuttering in fear, "he was arrested last night for beating up Giles' Dad."

"Tell Kieran, I will get him when he gets out."

More unfinished business, but he would hear about the murder of his family and could live in constant fear. I latched my fangs around Liam's ear and ripped it off for good measure. I left the room, stepping over the dead bodies and through the pools of blood, just as the credits on the TV rolled and the room plunged into darkness once more.

I heard no movement upstairs. I guessed they were used to the sounds of screams from the TV. I ascended to the women of the house as well, the Mum and the two sisters. They were no better having beaten up Giles' older sister and taken part in some of the other bullyings, smashing the house windows and prank calls. I would take more time with them.

"No, Jon. We are leaving," Thorn's thoughts entered into my head. I should have known Thorn wouldn't allow me to kill them.

I guessed the loss of their father and son or brother would be enough. I could always come back again. In the meantime, let them live in fear, just as I did for all those years.

Now, I only had one bully left to complete my revenge, Barry.

CHAPTER TWENTY-ONE

We returned to London the night after exacting revenge on the O'Keefes and resumed our regular pattern of training and hunting.

The next night back had been another eventful night out with Thorn hunting, as she had read reports of a gang of muggers working in a nearby park. We went to the park that night and pretended to be two young lovers hiding away in the bushes. They had seen us and circled, ready to take our money. Yet it didn't go according to plan, as she broke and fed on them. After my success in Leeds, I joined in and fought as a human against one of the men. I protected myself well and got in a few decent hits. I smiled, pleased with myself. I was growing with confidence and strength every time I fought.

Back at home, after the fight in the park, night drew to a close. Thorn was drifting off to sleep downstairs in the basement, and I sat by myself on the sofa sipping a cold drink, savouring another night with Thorn. Being away from Thorn, and the light coming through the windows, I felt myself changing. Night Jonathan's grip slipped away, and the nagging doubts and fears of Day Jonathan crept through into my thoughts. He questioned everything I had done over the last few nights, urging me to give up and let him prepare his escape plan and to dream of being back in Scarlett's arms once again. His voice argued with me, and war raged in my mind as the daylight came and Thorn slept.

"You were going to kill those O'Keefe girls," Day Jonathan said.

"They deserved it. They were just as bad as their brothers were. Don't you remember?" I replied.

"Of course, but they were asleep in their beds. They never hurt you. Maybe others but not you."

"Some others can't defend themselves. It's up to me to bring them to justice."

"That's not your job. You should have gone to the trial and not gotten mixed up with vampires. Justice would have been done."

"They always get away with it. You wanted the power just as much as I did at the beginning. You wanted to be free to walk in the day, not to be afraid anymore. You have that now," said Night.

"Maybe, but at what cost. People have died. Yes, the gang and the O'Keefes were bullies but did they deserve that? A beating maybe and prison but to be ripped apart, it wasn't right."

"But the slavers, we saved those girls," Night argued as his voice faded as the daylight grew brighter, and I could sense Thorn had drifted into a deep sleep.

"Yes, but the trail has run cold. Think of how many more could have been saved if they had been captured and imprisoned. Those girls saw you two rip those men apart. Those memories will haunt them as much as the abuse they suffered. Annabel and Lucinda are now in Thorn's pocket as well and will come to worse harm," I said, my voice growing stronger every passing minute as Day pushed Night away, and my body and face relaxed.

"But Thorn will protect us," he said.

"Like she was able to protect herself from being captured by the Hunters. You have been lucky up to now. Eventually, your luck will run out, and she will turn on you or fail you," I, Day Jonathan, said.

"No, I love her, she won't fail us."

"You are a fool. It's her powers you are in love with, not her. She made you fall in love with her. It's not real."

"It ... is," Night's voice whispered as he disappeared again for another day.

I took charge now, Day Jonathan and the daily passing and ritual of argument were finished again until Day receded and Night returned. My body had reverted to normal, muscles relaxed and the scowl on my face subsided to a natural state. The dark marks under my eyes faded away, and the skin regained its normal colour. The constant anger and adrenaline dispersed back to a calmer, more rational state of mind.

I went on the computer to practice the escape route home once more and noticed I had received an email from Annabel and Lucinda. The girls had settled in at Miss Jones's house and were to be enrolled in college at the start of the next academic year. While we hunted the O'Keefes, Thorn had employed them to keep an eye out for Barry, to lure him out of hiding. Thorn performed a makeover, so they would pass as eighteen and hired a driver to take them on a tour of night spots. She paid them well for the work, and they seemed happy to see Thorn again and be of use. The email told me that Annabel had attracted his attention on a night out and could arrange a date for us to capture him. They had scouted out the house of Barry's cousin, Terry, and the Hunters had gone. I arranged it for two night's time, giving us time to formulate a plan. At last, we could finish what I had started, and then I could escape Thorn's clutches.

I went upstairs and checked all parts of the escape plan were ready. I had found the spare keys to the BMW and had enough experience to drive it. I went into the loft to check the small rucksack with everything prepared, and that everything was still inside. In the bag was money, mobile phone to call ahead, a silver knife I had purchased from a pawnbroker, a UV light I had made myself, and finally the map of the route. I wanted the rest of the needles, but Thorn had locked them away in the safe in the walk-in wardrobe.

I went to practise the route once more on Street View, and I estimated it would take just over an hour. I couldn't leave the house until the afternoon, as it would be too out of the ordinary. I needed to stick to my regular routine for it to work, which would only give me three or four hours to return in the daylight. It should be enough, but I was preparing for any eventuality. As Day Jonathan, I looked forward to returning home and seeing Scarlett again, even if it meant betraying Thorn and leading the Hunters back to her.

#

The two days passed and the night we were taking revenge on Barry approached. The daylight receded, and I laid awake in bed next to Thorn. I was Day Jonathan with Thorn fast asleep and the sun lowering in the sky but could feel Night Jonathan creeping into my thoughts. I felt nervous and scared about what would happen tonight, but he felt excited and eager.

"Tonight is the night for our final revenge," he, Night Jonathan, said.

"Revenge doesn't mean we have to kill him," I said.

"It does. There is no other way. He knows what we are."

"True, but who would believe him anyway. Let's just give him a beating and tomorrow we can be free and back with Scarlett."

"Free, we are free, you idiot. Scarlett betrayed us, remember."

"No, I am sure she can explain. We can forgive her," Day's fading voice replied, and with it his overly emotional feelings and calmness.

"Explain! You are too soft. If you weren't such a pushover, none of this would have happened. You could have saved Giles at those gates," I, Night Jonathan said, and I could feel my muscles strengthening as the desire to take revenge took hold.

"No, we were outnumbered."

"So what? A few bruises and a couple of computer games would have been worth it to protect your friend. After everything he and his family did for you, when your own father was too busy to notice," I said.

"But, it wasn't like that."

"You are weak and pathetic. I despise you. Once Barry is dead, I am telling Thorn everything about your betrayal. I will ask her to help me get rid of you once and for all," I said.

"No ..." Day's voice trailed off into nothingness. My face had returned to normal, and I felt a scowl come across it as I prepared for the night's events.

"Thorn loves me, and I love her. Scarlett only ever betrayed us. No explanation can wash it away," I said, disgusted at his weakness, and there was no reply.

The light of the day had passed, and Thorn stirred from her sleep. Night pushed Day away, and I had changed again. I was Night Jonathan, and I wasn't interested at all in escaping and despised Day Jonathan for such weakness. I didn't want to see Scarlett again, as she had betrayed me with Barry. The images of them still burnt into my memory. Thoughts of another night with Thorn and the final destruction of Barry excited me. I looked forward to revenge and being a vampire again. My love for Thorn had consumed me. I enjoyed our life together. Why would I want to leave? I didn't care what Day Jonathan thought, as my love for Thorn was real.

Thorn smiled. "You talking to someone?" she asked, stretching out in bed.

"Just myself," I replied, and kissed her on the cheek.

I flitted back and forth as I chose my clothes and continuously changed the music, preparing myself for the mission. I wanted to wear the same clothes that I wore on the night I first turned into a vampire in the park, but I had grown through the three previous injections and the training. The jeans didn't fit anymore, too short and tight. I put on some new black jeans and a new pair of black boots. The black t-shirt I wore before used to hang off my weak body but now fitted snugly across my new muscles. I kept it on as I posed in front of the mirror. I was pleased with my developing body shape. The leather jacket also now fitted perfectly with my new muscles filling it out. As I looked at myself wearing the mix of old and new, I realised how far I had come. I knew tonight would reveal a new me, as I completed my revenge and freed myself from my fears.

This was a special night; the completion of our mission. Once my revenge had been exacted on Barry, we were free to leave London. I had to complete my training before I learnt more about vampires and could travel to her other houses across the world. I had to prove to Thorn that I was worthy.

Thorn bounced around the basement, trying on different outfits, until she decided on her black leather catsuit. I watched Thorn slide herself into the catsuit and pull on a pair of black shiny knee-high length boots. I walked over, knelt in front of her and squeezed the sides of the boot over the tongue. They squeaked and rubbed together as I laced up the boots on either leg.

"Thank you, darling," she said.

She applied black eye makeup, red lipstick and then sat on the edge of the bed, painting her fingernails black. She stood in front of the mirror, flicked her raven tousled hair about and waved her nails dry.

"Okay?" she said.

"Definitely," I responded.

I had never seen her as excited as this before, or dressed so provocatively. I guessed she wanted to be seen as a vampire tonight, to revel in the imagery and the myths. She liked to act the part.

We packed the car and drove to the meeting place, the alley where Barry and his gang had mugged me. We arrived, and Annabel was waiting in a car with the driver Thorn had employed.

As we watched, I tapped my fingers on the armrest, unable to contain the nervous energy twitching through my system. I pulled out a newspaper clipping from my jacket pocket, "Gang revenge attack," the headline read from the Leeds chronicle. It didn't describe the details enough for my liking but stated the police believed it was linked to a gang revenge attack. The O'Keefes had other enemies; other gangs in the area had their own motives. Although the police were surprised by the brutality of the assault. Thorn had gotten the newspaper clipping and insisted I kept it to relive the moment and enjoy the revenge.

"It will be a trigger for the future and a reminder of your true power," she had said.

It seemed like the right time to look at it again before we tackled Barry.

Movement, Barry shuffled down the alleyway and looked around for Annabel. Barry looked rougher than usual, his blond hair not shaven as cleanly as before, and his face carried a haunted expression with his forehead overhanging with a frown. He wore his usual black puffer jacket, jeans and boots. Annabel climbed out of the car.

"Barry, over here. I got us a lift into town," she said and waved him across.

Barry walked past Thorn's car and over towards Annabel. I opened the door behind, and he glanced around doing a double-take, head swinging back around again as he recognised me.

"You," he said in a panicked voice and ran for Annabel.

"Quick, get into the car," he shouted.

Annabel got in, shut the door and her car drove off. He stopped and turned around to see me approaching. Thorn had already raced around the outside of him, blocking his path in the other direction.

"Leave me alone," he said, hands out in front as I approached.

I marched on, happy to see his face full of fear.

"Remember this place, Barry?" I asked.

"Get lost," he shouted and ran away into the path of Thorn slinking along in her black leather catsuit. He gazed at her, lost for words, his fear replaced by the desire she ignited. She unzipped the front of the catsuit to create ample cleavage and walked towards Barry.

"Hi, can you help me? I'm lost," she asked.

"Yeah," he grinned at her, hypnotised and forgetting his current peril.

She walked up closer with her catwalk swinging hips and smiled. Barry grinned and looked her up and down, absorbing it all. Thorn walked right up to Barry and placed her hand on his arm, and then punched his jaw, knocking him unconscious. I walked back to the boot and opened it. Thorn slung him over her shoulder like an empty bag and ran over to the trunk, depositing him inside. I tied him up and got back into the passenger's seat. Thorn got in, smiled and started the car. We drove off with the stereo thumping out loud guitars as we screeched off down the road.

I watched the stars and the full moon flashing in and out of the trees and bushes as we drove at dangerous speeds through the countryside. I had become used to the way Thorn drove now. She drove like someone who couldn't die and had lightning-fast reactions.

I thought about what would happen after tonight ended, and what I would do the next day. In the morning, I would have to decide; stay with Thorn or leave and try to get back with Scarlett. Eventually, I had to decide who I was, Day or Night, Human or Vampire. Therefore, I had to choose Scarlett or Thorn.

For now, I just enjoyed the wind rushing in through the open window, and the music shaking the car as Thorn swung the car down the dark country lanes. I looked around at her. She smiled, cranked up the music and began singing along. I joined in, and we hurtled along the roads, enjoying the cool night air and revelling in anticipation of the events to come.

CHAPTER TWENTY-TWO

After half an hour's drive, Thorn turned the music off, and we pulled down a country lane. Then turned again and we bumped along for a few minutes down a rough track path until it ran out at a half-fallen down old wooden fence.

"Ready," Thorn said.

"Yes," I replied, and we leant across the inside of the car and kissed.

We got out of the car, walked around to the boot and opened it.

Barry was still out cold, and Thorn picked him up out of the boot. I grabbed the camera equipment, and we walked into the woods.

It had been raining during the day, and the mud squashed under our feet as we tramped through the undergrowth and trees. The full moon provided enough light to follow Thorn as she made light work of carrying Barry. Walking through the woods, her feet barely touched the ground before springing forwards, over the branches, mud pools and slippery roots. I slipped and squelched through the mud and tree roots behind her, desperately trying to keep her in sight. And in comparison, I felt like a clumsy oaf.

We reached a large circular area empty of trees and bushes in the middle of the woods, and the ground had a reasonable covering of grass. The open sky allowed the extra light from the full moon to illuminate our activities. Thorn kicked down a small wooden fence blocking our way, and it smashed across the clearing, leaving a gap for us to walk through. We tied Barry to a tree, set up the camera on a tripod and put a lantern next to him to give light during the filming. He started waking up and taking in his new surroundings. I grinned as he woke, and my excitement grew as I imagined my final vengeance.

Barry had stolen my chance of a normal life. I had started to make something out of my life, putting the events of Leeds behind me when he attacked me. I had taken care of the O'Keefes, and Barry represented the final piece of the jigsaw. I would make him suffer. The others got away with a quick and easy death. I would take plenty of time with Barry, torturing him with fear and pain in equal measures throughout the entire night.

"You!" he said.

"Me," I answered.

"You're vampires, aren't you?" he asked, looking at us both.

"She is," I pointed, and Thorn took a theatrical bow, "I can sometimes

The Birth of Vengeance

be a vampire."

"The injection!"

"Yes. Just worked it out, did you?"

"What do you want from me?" he said, trying to wriggle free of his bonds.

"Guess," I asked and pointed at the camera.

He looked up at Thorn.

"Make me a vampire. I would be much better at it than this wimp," he said.

I didn't expect that offer, but I was safe. We had a deal Thorn and me.

Thorn turned to me, scrutinised me and viewed my reaction. She seemed to be weighing me up. I recoiled in horror; she was actually taking this offer seriously. My whole world suddenly spun out of control, and it transported me back to being a scared teenager again. My stomach tightened as she looked at me, and I tried to think of something to say but couldn't.

She turned back to Barry again. "Why?"

He smiled, pleased his offer was being considered.

"I am ruthless and hard already. I would be your loyal servant. We could rule the night, you and I."

Thorn smiled, enjoying the attention.

She stared over at me again. "And you?"

I stared utterly stunned at her and Barry. "What?" I asked in a frightened voice.

"See, he isn't worthy of you," Barry said, enjoying the situation.

"Shhhh meat," she said to Barry and extended her finger to him.

"Why should I take you instead of Barry?" she asked.

My mind raced through the options. What was she looking for? What did she want? I didn't know what she wanted. All I knew was how I felt.

"Quickly." She pushed for an answer.

"Because, because," I stalled, "because I saved your life," I answered, and she nodded in agreement.

"And?" she said.

"We have a deal."

"And?" she asked again.

I looked down at the floor; what else could I say.

"And?" she repeated, crossing her arms.

Barry smiled and thought he had won. I had to say something, or all was lost.

"I love you," I murmured while staring at the mud, and I knew this was a worthless and pointless answer to a vampire.

"Louder," she said.

She must have heard. I looked up at her and stared straight into those sky bright eyes.

"I love you," I said again with confidence, meaning and passion.

She smiled at me, and her lips parted a little, showing her fangs just underneath.

"Good," she answered.

"See Barry, he loves me. You have your answer."

Barry seemed unsure, was this yes or a no?

"You, on the other hand, are a dull, mindless thug," she stated.

I breathed a sigh of relief; she had been playing with me.

"However, it could be interesting," she said, giving a twisted smile and a red glint flickered in her eyes. She walked over to Barry and loosened his bonds.

Barry smirked and wrangled free, getting quickly to his feet. I staggered backwards with my heart pounding, the woods spinning and her words echoing in my ears. I couldn't believe she had turned on me after everything we had been through. What happened to our deal? I suppose I shouldn't have been surprised, as she was a vampire, even so, it came as a shock. Thorn pulled out a knife and threw it into the middle of the clearing.

"Fight for me," she said, smiled and walked over to the side of the clearing next to the camera.

I looked about for an exit, and so did Barry.

"No running," she shouted, baring her fangs and claws as a warning.

Barry didn't hesitate, pushed me over and dived for the knife. He knocked me over as I recoiled from her shocking announcement, and I landed on my arse in the wet mud. The wet landing and sudden smack across my backside jolted me out of my shock. Barry picked up the knife and came back at me, smirking and throwing the knife hand-to-hand.

"New boy, time's up, no special drugs this time."

I grabbed part of the broken fence and jumped back onto my feet. Barry sliced the air before him and crouched down, ready to spring. I held the wood out in one hand as I prepared to block the knife. I didn't know what to do. In Leeds, when I hit Dave, I had Thorn just behind me. If it went wrong, she was there to protect me. All the other times as a human, Thorn was always there to rescue me or scare them off. At the nightclubs, she would step in at the last moment to save me from a beating. Even a couple of days ago in the park, I only fought one person who ran off after Thorn decimated the rest of his gang.

The other times I was a vampire; I had superior strength, speed and instincts. I didn't stand a chance against Barry. I knew it, and he knew it. Thorn must have known it, but I again reminded myself that she was a vampire, and I had allowed my love for her to cloud my judgement. Day Jonathan was right; I had to escape if I survived tonight.

Barry lunged, and I reacted to my surprise and blocked with the stick. He tried further slices and stabs, and I swung the stick in time to parry the blow or distract him from his task. Barry circled and charged, and I stepped to the side, moving out of reach. Again, he charged, and I stepped out of the way. I couldn't keep this going forever. I was just trying to survive, hoping that a miracle would happen else the outcome would be inevitable. Barry had a reputation that was how you became a gang leader, and he wasn't afraid of getting his hands dirty. I should know.

Again, he moved forward and stabbed at me. I backed off, swinging the stick. He followed with a stab and slice. He came forward again and again, and I circled backwards, thrusting the stick to block the knife.

"Come on, fight me," Barry shouted.

Thorn watched on, interested by the cat and mouse game, following our movements with the filming camera. Maybe I could just tire him out, and he would make a mistake. His face raged, and he wanted revenge for the death of his friends and fear he lived in since I killed them. I hadn't thought about his desire for revenge, just mine.

Again, we moved around each other in the centre of the clearing. Barry then kicked up a pile of leaves and dirt and charged in behind it, which distracted me as I shielded my face. He hit me full-on, and we crashed down into the mud.

Pain shot through my left shoulder, and I put my hands up to protect it. I was too late. I could feel the metal blade pushing through my flesh. I grabbed at the handle in Barry's hand, trying to push it out.

We rolled around in the mud, coating our clothes and faces and fighting for dominance over the blade. I couldn't push him away, but I was stopping it going in any further. We rolled again, and Barry was on top, his face full of fury, bearing his weight and strength onto the blade to drive it all the way in. I used all my strength to hold it steady, but I couldn't last forever. It was only a matter of time before it plunged through the rest of my shoulder. The pain would be too much, and he would cut me to pieces and take my place at Thorn's side.

"Boys," Thorn said, "Something extra." She threw a vampire formula needle onto the ground a few meters away.

We both looked over at it, and I wondered what to do next. Maybe if I could get to the needle, I could transform, and it would heal my wounds.

"New boy, when I am finished with you, I am going to take that needle and break your girlfriend."

I looked over at Thorn. He couldn't be serious. She would destroy him.

"I think Thorn can look after herself," I answered, looking at her.

"Not her, you idiot, the redhead," he said, laughing.

"No," I screamed into his face.

Memories of Scarlett flashed across my mind. The first time I met her in the sixth form common room and the elation of being introduced and becoming friends. My first kiss with Scarlett at her house, my heart hammering and feeling like it was breaking open my rib cage. After the mugging, Scarlett cradling my head, her tears dropping onto my face, and her flame hair billowing in the wind. After pushing her over at college, then the tears of heartbreak rolling out her green eyes and nose bleeding onto her lips. At the nightclub, saying I could still come home, and we could be together again. The hope it sparked and the rekindling of my love for her. Then it happened, the uncontrollable rage I felt when I became a vampire, but this was a pure human rage.

The anger brewed 'til boiling point, and my muscles shook with the rage. The blood rushing faster and faster around my body, heart pumping and hormones crashing about sparking every part of life force I had to sacrifice. My face went red, and I gritted my teeth from the change. I emitted a low intense growl that turned into a full ear-splitting roar, saliva spitting from my teeth and into Barry's face. The muscles around my hands squeezed tight, crushing his grip. The sudden strength in my arms pushed the blade out of my shoulder as I screamed into his face.

His expression changed as he lost the battle of strength between us. Fear crossed his face. My psychic abilities picked up images of me as a vampire in his mind. He thought I was changing. I wasn't. This was just old-fashioned human rage. Rage and anger inspired by my love of Scarlett. He had taken everything from me, and I wouldn't let him take any more.

The blade came out of my shoulder, and I pushed it to the side, allowing the pressure between us to be released. His head dropped with the lack of resistance, and I smashed my forehead into his nose. The blood spurted out as he screamed in pain. I didn't stop and grabbed his nose between my teeth, pulling and tearing. His blood poured into my mouth, and I gulped it down, imagining I was a vampire. Time to finish.

I pushed him off to the side of the clearing. Still in a rage, I got to my feet, but I was steady and thinking straight as I walked over to the needle. I had used my anger and love to fight back. I had bathed in my emotions, just as Thorn had taught me. However, I was Day Jonathan, as the thoughts of Scarlett had been overwhelming and had triggered the reactions I needed to win. This side of my personality had the strength to react and the motivation to fight. Day had won over Night. My face and body returned to its natural self, the scowl and the tenseness gone. I felt calm and in control of my emotions, not scared of my thoughts and feelings.

I picked up the needle and looked at Barry holding his nose and rolling around on the floor, moaning in pain. He knew what would happen next when I injected, and he watched, preparing for his last moments. I knew what would happen; the vampire would take charge, and the instincts would be strong. All I needed to do was let it off the leash. It would be easy for me. No pain. No thought required to kill Barry.

I turned to Thorn and threw the needle down by her feet instead. I wanted to feel all of it. To feel the pain on my knuckles. I didn't want it to be easy. I wanted to experience every single moment. For it to be under my control and to remember it as a human. Barry and I on the same level man-to-man. This was going to be my, Day Jonathan's, moment of triumph, and I didn't care if Thorn sensed the change in my emotions, or sensed my love for Scarlett. I had made my decision for better or worse.

Barry charged headfirst at the sight of the needle being thrown away. I stepped to one side, and powered a knee across my body and hit the side of his head. He crashed to the ground. Thorn's training had come to the fore; my confidence and aggression triggered the movements I had practised.

I slid the knife into the back of my jeans and clenched my fists, ready to practice some more. He got back on his feet, and I moved forward, prepared for contact. He swung a fist. I ducked and threw an uppercut onto his chin, and then swiped an elbow across his face, fracturing his cheekbone. Barry crashed to the ground, whimpering. I kicked him in the stomach, and he curled into the mud to cover up. I walked about him, kicking him in the back and legs as he tried to crawl away. After a while, I stopped, not wanting him dead, and dragged him to a tree. I pushed him against it, sitting him up. Blood poured out of his nose and from the cuts across his face.

I pulled out the knife, knelt down and looked into his eyes. I didn't intend to kill him. I didn't want to cross that line as a human, not now that I had decided who I wanted to be. Killing as a vampire was surreal, an out of body experience. This would be different and hard to cope with and recover from. I was Day Jonathan following the outpouring of emotions for Scarlett, and I wanted to return home as intact as possible. I had my revenge with the beating I had given him, but I wanted him to suffer for a bit longer by making him think I was going to kill him. I wanted to make sure he never came after me.

I remembered him talking to me about consequences, so I reflected his speech back on him.

"Life is all about consequences," I stated. "Consequences like mugging a new boy because you fancy his girlfriend. Consequences of me being in London in the first place, which is out of your control. The job my Dad does, or just simply looking the other way, has led us here tonight," I said and enjoyed my speech but could tell it went over his head.

"It's too late for you. Consequences, Barry, consequences," I said in a matter of fact voice and flicked the knife back and forth in the air. His eyes traced it as I waved it around and fear consumed his face.

"Don't kill me. It wasn't my idea. They paid me to mug and bully you," Barry blurted out.

"What!" I replied. I felt like someone had punched me in the stomach and the news rocked me backwards.

"Yeah, these guys paid me two-thousand pounds to give you a kicking. Then more money again on the Sunday night to carry on the following week," Barry said, hands held up in front of his body, surrendering.

"What people?" I asked as acid crept up my throat.

I wanted to be sick but forced it back down.

Thorn walked over, intrigued by what Barry just said.

"The people who will be here any minute," Barry said, laughing and looking around the woods.

I was confused. I didn't know what to do. So, I looked around, trying to sense anyone approaching, but could only hear the wind rustling the leaves in the trees and creaking of branch against branch.

"You mean the people who gave you this, Barry," Thorn said, holding up a small broken plastic box.

Barry padded his jacket in a frenzy but to no avail.

"Yeah," he said defeated, looking at her hand with the box.

"A transmitter. I broke it when I first captured him," Thorn replied.

"Who?" I asked.

Barry didn't answer but just looked down at the mud, defeated and broken.

"Who?" I said again, waving the knife under his nose.

"The same guys who had been sniffing around ever since you killed my friends. They have been talking to everyone. They paid for the attacks on you and the bullying. They gave me the transmitter to track you down. It was all arranged, the mugging, the bullying and your girlfriend," Barry said.

"Thorn?"

"No, Scarlett, they wanted you to suffer as much as possible."

His words stunned me, and I tried to work out what it meant. The sickness burnt away in my stomach, distracting me from my thoughts.

Thorn interrupted. "She is part of it, building you higher than you have ever been, so the fall would be further, harder and darker. Enough to make you take the vampire formula. No wonder the Hunters were at the nightclub waiting when we saw Scarlett."

I had been played from the beginning. There was no random consequence. They, the Hunters, planned it all, but it had gone wrong. I had come back, released Thorn and taken the needles. They wanted the needles and me back for testing. Barry was involved, my Dad and Scarlett as well.

That would explain why a woman like Scarlett ever went out with me in the first place. I always knew she was too good for me. I was just a scrawny depressed teenage boy, and she was a beautiful young woman.

It all made sense now. The special attention and introduction from the Headmaster. Then being introduced to Scarlett on the first day was no accident, plus all those shared lessons. She just pretended to like me. The same music and film tastes, and we came from the same place as well. The constant chasing me about college when I avoided her. The invite to her house when we started dating. She made all the moves and flirted, encouraging me onwards. Of course, it was her idea to walk out through the front gates where Barry and the gang were waiting. She dropped her bag, so I tripped up, and then she ran off until I was attacked.

I guessed I was supposed to use the injection sooner but didn't. Scarlett came around on that Saturday and started the argument in the hope it would trigger me into action. When that didn't work, they used the photo of her and Barry to tip me over the edge. Her final betrayal.

The memories flooded back, with my new insight putting them into the perspective of how I had been played. This was the truth of Scarlett. Thorn had been right about Scarlett at the nightclub with the Hunters waiting for me. Scarlett knew what I had done and tried to convince me to come back. The signs had always been there, and it made sense now when I looked back and viewed it correctly. She was always out of my league. I should have realised it was too good to be true. I had always known it was but enjoyed it anyway, and now the reality had come back to haunt me. I was an idiot.

The memories triggered other disturbing truths. My Dad bringing me to the lab that night, knowing there was a vampire in the other room and letting me see the needles. It all fitted into the stories Thorn had told me about the lab and what thoughts she heard. It was a setup. They had purposely let her listen to their thoughts and set the needles down for me to see them and for her to tell me to take them. Why else leave an innocent and angry teenager next door to an imprisoned beautiful psychic vampire? It was all planned to test their formula in the field, and I wondered how far it went back; Leeds, the car accident, the bullying in school and obviously the new job. The half-packed boxes of books at the Leeds house and the waiting job offer the next morning after the O'Keefes' attack. The whole thing planned in detail.

I couldn't believe my own father had sold me out. My normal life destroyed. There would be no return, no happy ending and no dream life with Scarlett. The exact people who I thought could save me and give me a normal life again had put me here in the first place. They had been behind the scenes manipulating events to turn me into a test subject. I could only trust Thorn. She had been loyal to me every step of the way. Even tonight, I had realised as I fought Barry, it was part of the training. A test that she knew I would pass stronger than before. She had said at the outset it would be tough, and now I understood.

The tears burnt down my face as the extent of the betrayal sank in. My life was just an experiment. I was just a test subject. A line of data to measure results against.

"Why trick someone into using it? Why not pay someone?" I shouted at Barry.

He just shook his head. "I don't know."

"Take us to them," I told Barry as I choked on my tears.

"I don't know who they are. They would just appear from nowhere," he answered.

I felt numb and cold. My heart had been frozen solid, and it pumped ice into my veins. The tears had stopped, and the sickness went, but nothingness replaced it. Cold, empty, nothingness. My soul was void of thoughts or emotions. The stark reality of the truth had blown them away.

"You are of no use to me then," I said and thrust forward with the knife.

"No," he screamed as the knife penetrated his flesh.

I took Barry's life away. He screamed, and I saw Day Jonathan instead. It spurred me on. I stabbed harder, and I repeated it over and over again, taking in every moment of the flesh resisting the knife. The squelching of his stomach breaking as the knife tore at the fat and muscles. I enjoyed watching the hallucination of Day Jonathan dying and with it, his stupid dreams of redemption and forgiveness. His ridiculous fantasies of a normal life with Scarlett. His plans of escape and his potential betrayal of Thorn.

Thorn was the only real and loyal friend in everything that had happened. I loved her. The blood poured out over the knife, covering my hands in its sticky warmth and spurting onto my clothes. I was left now, Night Jonathan. No, even he had gone. I hadn't returned to Night Jonathan. My muscles and face remained the same, and the twitching energy hadn't returned either. Something inside had died and I remained void of any emotion. I'd become someone else, someone stronger, someone darker, but I wasn't sure who yet. I had regained my motivation and confidence in that battle, but the truth of the betrayal had hardened it into something solid and dark.

I stood up, watching my life as Jonathan Harper die beneath me, and then Thorn rushed over and hugged me.

"You are ready. You are my man. You passed the test," she whispered in my ear and kissed it, "we will find them, find the people who did this to you and the people who captured me, and we will get you answers and have our revenge."

I stared silently at Barry/Jonathan dying in front of me and tried to work out who I was and what my life meant.

"Jonathan, you will be okay. Trust me," Thorn said, putting her arm around my waist.

"Jonathan is dead," I said.

"You have chosen a new vampire name?"

"V."

Thorn looked at me.

"I am Vengeance," I answered.

"Yes, you are. Tonight you are reborn as Vengeance," Thorn said, and smiled.

We embraced and kissed as Barry's life drained away to the side of us.

Thorn pulled back.

"V, before he dies, may I."

"Yes," I answered and offered his blood to her by gesturing towards his dying body.

It seemed only right that Thorn should feed on his blood before he died.

"I love you," Thorn said. Her eyes gleamed, and I believed her.

Her fangs sprung out, and she was a blur as she locked onto his neck.

I watched Thorn feed, and I felt the vengeance and fury burning in my body, making me new, making me whole and turning me into Vengeance. I imagined my revenge on those who had betrayed me. I would find Scarlett and my Dad, and I would make them suffer.

Thorn flew backwards across the clearing and smashed into a tree. The leaves shook loose and fell onto her body. I looked back, and a needle stuck out of the side of Barry's stomach. His body started contorting, muscles spasming and flexing. He wasn't going to give up. I guessed he wanted his life back. Damn, he must have remembered where I threw the needle and crawled over to it. I grabbed the knife out the back of my jeans, and I just hoped Thorn would recover in time.

Barry's muscles on his one side kept getting bigger and bigger out of proportion with the rest of his body. His jaw extended out, and teeth broke out all over the place. His head enlarged, and flesh bubbled across his body. He hadn't turned into a vampire. The transformation had gone horribly wrong.

Instead, a lopsided enraged monster writhed on the ground. He lumbered to his feet and screamed at the full moon, staggering forward like a wounded animal. His flesh and muscles bubbled and contorted as the transformation spiralled out of control. He lumbered forward towards Thorn's limp vulnerable body to finish her off. Thorn is everything to me; she is my true love, and I am her saviour and protector.

"Over here," I shouted, jumping up and down, waving my arms.

It worked, and he lumbered away from Thorn and towards me. He had no idea who he was facing. I am Vengeance. He threw a massive swipe at my head, and I ducked, but he clipped my arm, and I flew across the clearing and onto the wet, muddy ground. I couldn't get close to him. He was too strong. One hit and it would be all over.

Thorn lay out cold against a tree. I would have to do this by myself. I got up and ducked numerous swipes. All the time, the transformation carried on and his body erupted in muscle and bone. The transformation slowed him down, and he stumbled and screamed again in pain at the full moon.

I saw my chance and ran for the camera tripod, grabbed it and headed back to the monster. I circled around his back and avoided the next punch. I coiled the tripod behind my back and smashed it across his skull. He stumbled, and I repeated the attack, breaking the tripod into shattered pieces of metal that embedded into his bones. His head broke open and blood poured out, but he kept moving on instinct and rage alone.

I pulled the knife out of the back of my jeans and launched into a stabbing frenzy into his chest. His monstrous blood and puss sprayed out, soaking me in a shower of sickening fluid.

He staggered back but regained his footing and lurched forward again. He seemed unstoppable. I tried to think of what to do next when Thorn crashed into the side of his body, ripping, tearing and smashing away in a terrifying cycle of claws and fangs. I had never seen her give everything, and I realised how powerful and dangerous she really was.

The monster's body broke down under the severity of the damage. The physical construct of his body giving up as it distorted and grew, the seams of its skin tearing apart. Flesh and bones erupted onto the floor and bubbled and contorted on its own.

An arm broke off, and his jaws ripped off under Thorn's attack. The damage reached a critical point, and the monster exploded across the clearing. I ducked and covered my hands across my face to shield it from the flying flesh. Thorn flew backwards again but landed and rolled out of the way. The monster's head fired into the trees, smashing the lantern and plunging the clearing into darkness.

I took a deep breath. The full moon came to my rescue, providing enough light to make out shapes and figures moving about. In the light of the full moon, Thorn picked herself off the ground and made sure the monster was dead.

Lumps of flesh and bone bubbled and contorted in piles of atrocious mess that covered the clearing. It dripped down from the trees and splattered against the tree trunks, dissolving the bark on contact. Steam rose from the piles of flesh and bone, and it stunk worse than off meat.

I turned my face away in disgust. Why didn't the formula work on him? Maybe it was just a bad batch, and I had been lucky before, or I was special. Hence all the effort into making me test it. Yet more questions I had for the people behind my betrayal.

The clouds swept across the sky, masking the full moon, and the clearing dived into pitch darkness. I couldn't see my hands in front of my face, but I felt the blood dripping off them. I stood in silence in that dark place.

Light footsteps sounded behind me, and a rush of wind breezed across my back. Thorn's hot hand slipped into my bloodied one.

"V, you are my protector, my saviour," she said and brushed the mud and tears away from my face, and kissed my stained cheek.

She pulled at my hand, but I stared into the darkness, frozen to the spot. "We can't stay here, my love."

"I want my revenge, and I want to know if the formula is safe," I said.

"You need to learn about the wider world and your place in it now that your training is complete. There are people who can help us," she said. "Come, V, I have a brand new world to show you. The truth of the vampire world and the riches it offers await. It will help you understand and help us plot our revenge. Something big is happening with this vampire formula that required such deception. Our destinies are bound together for a reason," she said.

I relaxed and looked away.

"V, follow me," she said in a low soft voice and walked away again.

Thorn led the way, and I followed her, hand-in-hand, into the darkness.

THE END

Eager to know where Thorn takes Jon next?

What awaits Jon in the rest of the vampire world?

Who is behind the vampire formula conspiracy?

Well, you don't need to wait for book 2, it's out now.

The Truth of Vengeance - Vampire Formula #2

Book Description:

"On the run and in the shadows, the life of a killer is bleak indeed. Jon Harper is no more, and the soulless shadow he has become lingers in the darkness, craving solace and answers. In order to make sense of his past and the creature he has become, V must seek out another vampire, Cassius. With his dangerous lover and sole companion, Thorn, by his side, V must venture into the unknown in an attempt to make sense of his actions.

So what is the truth behind vampires? What is the purpose of this dark, strange and destructive creature V has become? Will the truth set him free—or is his salvation shrouded in shadow as well?

Dive back into the heart of darkness in P.A. Ross' dark fantasy series Vampire Formula in this all new thrilling sequel that will leave you thirsty for more. Embrace the darkness and grab your copy of The Truth of Vengeance today!"

Printed in Great Britain
by Amazon